JO HAMYA

Three Rooms

VINTAGE

1 3 5 7 9 10 8 6 4 2

Vintage is part of the Penguin Random House group of companies whose
addresses can be found at global.penguinrandomhouse.com

Penguin
Random House
UK

First published in Vintage in 2022
First published in hardback by Jonathan Cape in 2021

penguin.co.uk/vintage

A CIP catalogue record for this book is
available from the British Library

ISBN 9781529114416 (B format)

Printed and bound in Great Britain by Clays Ltd, Elcograf S.p.A.

The authorised representative in the EEA is Penguin Random House
Ireland, Morrison Chambers, 32 Nassau Street, Dublin D02 YH68

Penguin Random House is committed to a sustainable future
for our business, our readers and our planet. This book is made
from Forest Stewardship Council® certified paper.

MIX
Paper from
responsible sources
FSC
www.fsc.org
FSC® C018179

I. 'There was another ten-shilling note in my purse; I noticed it, because it is a fact that still takes my breath away – the power of my purse to breed ten-shilling notes automatically. I open it and there they are. Society gives me chicken and coffee, bed and lodging, in return for a certain number of pieces of paper which were left to me by an aunt, for no other reason, than that I share her name.'

II. 'Instead of being serious and profound and humane, one might be – and the thought was far less seductive – merely lazy minded and conventional into the bargain.'

III. 'Clearly the mind is always altering its focus, and bringing the world into different perspectives.'

A Room of One's Own,
Virginia Woolf (1929)

PART ONE

'You no longer possess your own furniture'

I.VI

My first experience of the house was shuttling boxes through the front door. The place stood solid, and in the process of moving in, I kept leaving it.

I wanted to lend rhythm to this – establish pattern and pace to the lunge of my back with kitchenware and books in the front garden's hot air; the release of setting them down inside. I took boxes in: those went to a single room. On my desk someone had left the receipt for rent and a five-week deposit, a tenancy form; they'd arranged the washed-out furniture and given instructions for the accompanying inventory rigmarole. Then I took my body out, and the building was visible as a whole – brick-work, disused chimneys, roof. Boxes in: their unmade, jigsaw rattle of stuff; my body out: Victorian Gothic, and the garden's hedges carefully pruned. I wanted to work with the dichotomy of things: the constant present tense of the house, and the vision I had of myself, unpacked, future perfect. But within ten minutes I had decided this was an exhausting way to live, and so I let myself separate. The house without my body, before its easy chairs and standing lamp, before its mirrors and branded sheets, fridge and food that filled it, could be imagined like this:

Squares of walls, large windows, blue carpets, sinks. Then the light fixtures. The skirting boards, plug sockets, radiators, curtain rails, bookshelves built into the walls. The building was just modern and moneyed enough to have had some version of the radiators and the incandescent light bulbs when it was originally built, but the plug sockets must have come later. Over time, such features had been replaced with updated versions of themselves. These were the rooms in question, but what they belonged to had its own skeleton, too: three floors, several corridors, a basement of servants' quarters, gardens. Now, over the original cedar, the stairs had white-washed banisters and the carpets got dirtier each year. Time filled it in and emptied it out again, but the house had been built to a different purpose and had gone gracelessly grey. The rent changed hands. Strange things happened to the building. The attic could not have held one cramped, slanting bedroom in its origin. The kitchen must have been in the servants' quarters, not the ground floor, where a living room should evidently have been. Now there was no living room. Gradually, the place lost the semblance of a grand home, and then of a family home, and then of a home altogether, if such a thing could be distinguished by way of coherence and permanence. The basement got sealed off and furnished in IKEA with a studio conversion in mind. The curtain rails were hung with bland, cheap fabric, an offence to the building's nineteenth-century facade; bits of the bathroom shone plastic – they might have been porcelain in another time. But the ugliness of this went unopposed: room tenancies in the house

4

lasted less than ten months. The whole that persisted, the building itself, was made up of eight contracts per academic year. Each room became a discrete abode.

Like this, it should have been nothing special. But at some point, outside, on the wall where the front door was, the house had acquired a blue plaque. The plaque read: 'You can put your things in one of these rooms, sure. You can take your cups and your shoes and your toothbrush out of cardboard boxes and arrange them all until it smells like what you are used to: old coffee, fabric softener, Diptyque candle – *feu de bois*. You can cut your nails, roll up your stockings, have sex, refill your fountain pen, count out spare change, eat figs, swat flies, stain the carpet, have an existential crisis (then shelve it for another day), shave, apply mascara. Now that it is the twenty-first century, you can send a tweet, read a reprint of Hegel, eat Chinese take-away made by English caterers on minimum wage; you can update your Instagram story, spread almond butter on rye-bread toast, stare at your MacBook, and generally *exist* in here to the tune of a £550 deposit and the sum of £187 in weekly rent, but always, *always*,

Walter Pater
1839–1894
Author and Scholar

Clara Pater
1841–1910
Pioneer of Women's Education

Lived here
1869–1885

Essentially it said, 'Fuck you.'

I lived in a borrowed room.

This was North Oxford, Bradmore Road. The house now served as a repository for postdoctoral research assistants at the university. When I moved my boxes in, the only thing to be heard on TV and the radio and online was that Britain was still leaving the EU. The leaving had been going on for a while. It was being done by old Oxonians whose former quarters I now rented for a nine-month period. The news beating out from every device in the country came in a language of rooms: a house called Number 10, borders, backstop, more Houses, this time of Commons and of Lords. It seemed to me that even the highest echelons of power existed by virtue of their quarters; would be loath to give them up. I supposed it was not an entirely illogical proposition. Perhaps what the rampant racism, anti-immigration policy and classism came down to was an arbitrarily powerful group of people wanting to preserve a world which could birth them into secure rooms; give them dorms in Eton and Oxford, chambers in Westminster, then a pension and country house to retire in. My brain did various contortions like these around this year, trying out excessive sympathy and rage like outfits in a changing room, to see which could make the most sense of the country around me. Nevertheless, the internet kept me reliably informed in other ways. A search via Google told me that the Department of National Statistics cited loss of rented accommodation as a key factor in the 4% yearly rise in homelessness. I joined a Facebook group dedicated to calculating the increased severity of austerity through the rising cost of Freddos. Every now and then, the outline of a west London council flat diminished, then surged over a horizon of digital headlines – not forgotten, until it was, and then remembered again. From what I understood, Brexit was to result in the erection of a stronger British State, but every article I found read the same: September 2018 may well have been June 2016. Nothing changed, and though I taught myself bits of political and legal jargon scribbled down from the news, the government's output remained oracular in my life – vague in meaning; difficult to apply. This seemed to be the case for most others. Pundits and parliamentary conversation moved in circles. Twitter offered vox pops. It became clever for news media to say they had no idea what was going on. I sympathised. Each time I scrimped and saved, swapped a £2.35 Americano for a 99p filter coffee, the grand irony of paying close to £10,000 to take up rooms in a place responsible for spawning the government that daily diminished my ability to afford a mortgage or the cost of rent was not lost on me. It was all, generally, going to hell.

On the morning of my arrival, I left my boxes unpacked and did a loop around town. From St. Giles' on, buildings rose in spires above me. Students touched key fobs to old wooden doors. On the High Street, I saw myself reflected in shop windows, colleges across the road thrown back behind me: my silhouette, some shades darker than the honeycomb.

It turned out that like most places in England, Oxford could be toured in the manner of history one paid to choose. Broad Street held clusters of people who all took the city according to their particular interest. The tour guides held up boards announcing each theme: wartime

Oxford, literary Oxford, famous Oxford alumni, Morse, historic alehouses, Past Present and Future Oxford, science trail, C.S. Lewis and J.R.R. Tolkien, *X-Men*, children's tours, Women at Oxford University, carvings and codes in stone, 'uncomfortable' tours where the group could choose to hear about the city's history of imperialism, wealth and social inequity, anti-Tory tours, pro-Tory tours, bus tours, walking tours, college tours, Anglican tours, Christian tours, tours in simple admiration of Christopher Wren. It didn't matter whether the history was real or not. A quick headcount was all it took to establish that Harry Potter was the most lucrative option. I thought, perhaps you should take one – but the uniformity of tourist backpacks and lanyards dangling passports made each of them indiscriminate to me. By the time I'd come back to St. Giles' the whole place had turned into a set of carefully designed, overlapping fabrications. Students' young, harassed-looking faces made their way around selfie sticks produced by visitors who transmuted bits of the city to each other in Polish or Japanese. There were as many Oxfords as the languages into which it could be spoken and phones into which it could be seized; then cropped, filtered, hashtagged, and released for replication on screens in locations further away. At the cusp of the city centre, groups of day trippers and schoolchildren got off buses and boarded them again, ferried in and out for intermediary stretches of time, believing that this, too, could be theirs.

I got back to the house and found that I had left the window open. There were wasps crawling over it, sluggish with the heat. Some had made it in, but others struggled with entering the room. They had not found the gap between pane and lower frame and tossed their bodies slowly at the glass. To those dull little thudding sounds I completed the inventory, taking photos at various angles with my iPhone's camera. When this was done, I unpacked. Within an hour, all my things were arranged and I could begin to think of the room as mine. I opened the window further still to let as many wasps out as I could. The rest, I killed with a book wrapped in a tea towel, propping open the door to give them as good a chance of escape as possible. Soon, a bespectacled face appeared before it.

I'm the room across from yours, it said. Cup of tea?

And I panted, I'd love to, I just want to get rid of these; gestured at the wasps which became more agitated with each blow. Two of them had abandoned the window and begun hurling themselves around at high speed. I said to the face, There's a kettle just there, please come in, I won't take long – to which a full body came into view and solicitously set about filling the kettle to its brim. This was how I met my neighbour. I waved the towel in the direction of cups and tea bags and went back to my own task. It was a large room with high ceilings. It was perfectly formed for a wasp not to be killed. I gave up with the book and began flicking the tea towel so that it snapped like the sail of a ship beating against the wind. Eventually things stilled. The room had come with easy chairs. I took a seat, and motioned that he should do the same.

Awful, aren't they? he commiserated. I've got several staking a claim in mine. He moved his head in the direction of his room, then added as an afterthought: We

9

should make them pay rent, and laughed at his own joke. You've got a lot of things, he pointed out and peered at the bookshelf. Lots of books.

I told him, Yes, they make the room look pretty. In fact, they did, but he gawped at me. I tried not to laugh and explained that I had taken my degrees in English. He asked if I was working on anything he'd have read. Because of how genial he was, I thought there was something old-fashioned about him. My guess was that he would have reclined in his seat even if he hadn't been in an easy chair, and he held the mug he'd found on my shelf comfortably by its handle as though he'd been drinking from it his whole life. He asked whether I'd been a postdoc assistant before. I had not, I said. I thought I'd try it for a year and see whether the job market eased. I had secured my position after almost a year of unemployment; had sent out dozens of applications a week, landing just enough fixed-term minimum wage and freelance work to survive. Occasionally, my parents had helped me, but this had come with its own strings: alongside their verbal agreement that it was more difficult for young people than it had been for them, was the unspoken sense that there was an expiry date for me to get myself together by. And since they had been financially independent at my age, had bought a house, what I felt I needed at the very least was a stable job. The probability of one seemed to eternally decrease.

My neighbour's face turned reassuring. I wouldn't worry about that, he said. Everyone and their mother has a doctorate now, it makes teaching posts really hard to find. You'll get good experience doing this anyway. He smiled at the expression on my face and leaned over to pat my hand. The academic market will be oversaturated for a while. But if they keep driving tuition prices up, in a generation or two, we might stand a chance. We'll just have no one to teach.

I shook my head. I meant a job in the real world. He cocked his at me; asked, Why on earth would you want to go near that?

I felt too stupid to reply. At that point, it was still too intimate to tell this stranger that the end goal I wanted, through any job necessary, was to be able to afford a flat, not just a room, and then to settle in it and invite friends to dinner. I thought I had put reasonable effort into this desire through successive degrees while waiting for the economy to clear up enough to raise the median starting wage. But the morning's news cycle and the job alerts I'd set up over email delivered the same disheartening report each day. Now, even to me, it seemed ridiculous to concede that I had accumulated substantial debt and a few degrees so that I might contractually labour for the sake of having two free days a week in which to cook a meal in a kitchen I could not actually afford to own, for a small crowd of people my age who spent their lives doing the same.

I pretended that what he had said could be construed as a joke instead, and smiled. I wanted to change topic, and thought I could do so by asking what research project he was attached to. I said, What about you? But my neighbour looked perturbed. Me? No, I don't want to look at any job outside of this, it's horrible out there.

I agreed, but my question had been about what it was he did now. He said, Ah, of course, as though this were evident, but I couldn't quite see why. It was clear to me that what I'd asked had misfired because he could not hear the conversation I had been having in my head, which took a different speed to the one I was having with him. I wanted to discuss this, but he'd already set about telling me that he belonged to the philosophy faculty. This was his third year there; his original contract had been extended by an additional twelve months, and when that had finished, he had attached himself to a new project with another research fellow in the department. He took a sip of tea and reverted to me: if I didn't want to stay in academia, what kind of job would I do instead?

Something where language has practical value, I said.

You mean – he was getting frustrated – something where it can be adequately monetised?

I knew this was not what I'd meant. But it was hard to argue with something that made so much brute sense. I told him words were the first port of meaning, you couldn't put a price on them. He took a book from a nearby shelf and said, These happen to be priced at twenty-five quid. He tried to reach for another but I said, Yes, all right, and he settled back down with his tea. He made a face; asked, What's so special about the real world, then? Why would being here be less real than anything else? And I supposed that universities were a kind of incubation period. You stored up theories about life and then you took them outside to see whether they worked. I said, Don't you think it's important to go out beyond this? Now it was his turn to be able to construe what I'd said as a joke as well. He nodded towards my bookshelves again and asked, Have you read this Pater chap?

I resented the turn of subject for the sake of the conversation's ease. But yes, I had, and added that his sister was impressive too. She dealt in languages, taught Greek to Virginia Woolf so that Woolf might hear the birds better.

He hadn't read any Woolf; he wasn't sure what I meant. But he'd been seeking a way to make a connection between us land and added that I could tell him about Greek birds and the Paters sometime, at which I faltered. I knew the Paters had lived in Oxford but I had always imagined them in wood-panelled rooms in a college elsewhere. It hadn't occurred to me that they might have lived *here*, where I was to live, too – where there were floors to be swept and windows to be cleaned, where the accomplishments of their lives were carried out in tandem with boring, ordinary things. But the impression formed. Clara and Walter: eating breakfast, untucking sheets, locking the front door. Suppose something probable, like porridge after waking up to the cold. If I made porridge and let the smell of oats and milk waft through the corridor, would time collapse in on itself and allow me to glimpse the house both as it was now and as it truly was in its origin? Did such things leave a memory; was it possible to imagine the permeability of time in a room?

My neighbour said likely not, and sixteen years wasn't that long to spend in one house.

I was confused. Of course it was.

He put his tea down and tried not to look sad. Did it seem like a long time to me?

This was the last of the morning. Outside, the light hit the tips of the trees, then diminished further down each trunk, blocked out by the shadow of the house. The garden grew outwards, further away from the building where the sun had better reach. He let the silence hang and waited for me to speak. When I didn't, he offered, My parents have lived in their house for almost thirty years.

This forced me into deeper silence still. His words voyaged around the room and found nowhere to settle. Seeming to realise this, he made to stand. My room is the one across from yours, he informed me again. I play guitar, so if it gets loud just let me know. You can knock any time. He stopped at the door. I'm going out for a formal tonight, if you want to come.

I shook my head. I had already been told to save my evening for a meet and greet with the English faculty. It would be postgrads and teaching fellows, mostly. My neighbour smiled. You won't like it, he said. I told him I might. You won't like it, he repeated. I suppressed the urge to scream and smiled back instead.

All the same.

All right, he said. Well, when you get bored, come after.

We swapped phones. He tapped his number onto my screen, and in exchange, I made myself into numbers on his, too. He waved it in the air as confirmation of receipt. He left the room so easily I began to dislike him a little less.

Sink and unframed mirror. The south-west corner of the room. My phone, propped up between the faucet and the wall, and my lips in the mirror, and my fingers doing their little tap, tap over them with a tissue, blotting lipstick. All to the sound of my mother: Do we think that dress is the right choice for a work party, and my mother, Did you make sure they got the inventory form, and my mother, Are you making friends, and my mother, I miss you, when will you come home? The soft little worries running alongside the tap. I let them go down the plughole. It wasn't enough. Some aspect of them stayed, as though they'd filtered from the faucet into the glass of water I'd had before leaving for the meet and greet. I got lost on the way to the English faculty and ended up late.

When I found it, from the outside, the building looked like a Bond lair. The whole thing was designed in rectangles by someone who had evidently misunderstood the purpose of Brutalism. For all its sparseness, the building radiated luxury. Rooms done in glass and dark wood spoke, sonorous through their large open windows. The thrum of conversations trickled out leisurely, unhurried. It spread itself out over the building's brickwork and its flat roofs. The whole thing made no attempt to disguise its status as a new-build; threw itself still further into the role by sitting at odds with a decrepit church and silent, adjacent cemetery. I crossed the road and looked at the graves of well-known men whose afterlife it was to watch their work occasionally reinterpreted, but for the most part ignored by twenty-somethings on the pavement opposite. I found Pater's grave, then resumed my own place on the other side of the street.

The party could be characterised as one only by the sight of a drinks table around which various huddles had formed, each member clutching a glass of champagne. Everything had the air of being slightly stretched. The leather on the sofas shone too brightly, as though strained. The floorboards were bare. Nevertheless, someone had taken great pains to decorate. Noticeboards with numbers for help centres and bits of poetry had been spread all over the walls; there was a placard, and it read – 'Join OxfordConnect today for alumni and student events. Available via Apple and Android.' I looked around and in my long, thin red summer dress, immediately felt overdressed; I took my cardigan from my waist and wrapped it around myself. Everyone had already latched onto someone else in the room, and looked as though they had no intention of leaving their particular group now that it had been formed. People asked each other their names, plugged them into search bars. I found a gap in a huddle of students and approached the formation from the side, angling my body half in, half out. I could be ready to leave should they decide they did not want me. A tall brunette girl held the stem of her champagne glass while two boys asked her who she was.

I'd slid in in time to hear that her name was Ghislane.

The boys looked at each other, their heads began to sway. *O-o-o Ghislane. One day she'll find her fame*, they sang. The girl winced.

Bet you get that all the time, said one of the boys, clearly delighted. She tipped the remainder of her glass down her throat and said, Fuck off, into it with some dignity. They did not. Ghislane fixed on me. I think I recognise you, she said. You were walking around town earlier.

She had widely spaced eyes and a long, broad nose. She chewed on her small, wet lips and waited for an answer. With her schoolgirl skirt and turtleneck, with her tailored jacket and darting, impatient gaze, she looked somehow very grown-up and not grown-up at all. There were probably only three years between us. Standing before her made me feel inexplicably unsophisticated.

I told her it was possible, yes.

Okay, she said, accepting her escape route and guiding me towards a table with more champagne. A hand at the small of my back, a steer and request: Please let's get away from them.

I was trying to pick up the pace. What was that song they were singing with your name in it? I asked.

She winced again. *Ghislane*. Stupid song from the nineties about a guy whose girlfriend leaves him to be a fame whore or whatever. The MeToo movement should have killed it except someone made an argument about female agency, so it lived to fight another day. Then someone – a man, obviously – began moaning that it was just an objectively good song and that we – she crooked her fingers in air quotes around the word *we* – should be allowed to sing it as long as we recognise it as *of its time*. Really, you've never heard it?

I shook my head. This earned me a look of admiration.

It actually is meant to be a classic. Sad girls on the internet quote it when they want to look deep. She passed me a glass of champagne.

That seems like an unfortunate thing to share a name with. I was trying to sound sympathetic, but she shook her head and said no-o-o. The syllable went up in impossible crescendo. It echoed the tune of what the boys had sung earlier. Ghislane fixed me with a firm look: in fact, she *was* named after it. Having established this, she examined me more closely. What did I do?

I told her. She asked, Do you think you'll be seeing a lot of everyone here? But I didn't know, so she began to point out others in the room with impressive flippancy.

What you're looking at is mostly contemporary lit. Our year is supposed to be some grand experiment, she said. They went for as many kinds of different people as they could. Apparently, our research proposals are all over the place. They want to see if they can breed the next great generation of literature. So...she considered the room over the rim of her glass. Then her mouth became a pistol, firing off bullets in expert shots: they're non-binary and gave a proposal on reading the canon as genderless; he's on anti-depressants doing environmentalist lit; she's queer; *she's* autistic, doesn't speak, but a total genius; he's obviously a Tory but he's working on something he's called 'literature for the working class', whatever the fuck that is; she's a sweetheart, but she says she gets terrible SAD, so I'm guessing she won't be much fun once the weather turns...and she's really annoying, don't talk to her. She glanced around the room to make sure everyone was accounted for, then pointed at herself brightly: Oh, and I have ADHD. So, yeah! What about you? Have you been here long?

I felt incredibly tired. I thought about it, catalogued what might be most true in my head, but all I had to offer up was the fact that I had been in London before. And of course, Ghislane said, you're BAME. She delivered the pronouncement with great solemnity. It was good that I was here. She'd come from London, too. Did I miss it? I shook my head. I was too recently gone.

Ghislane put down her flute. Sometimes, she said, she would take a night bus back. She got restless. She had

18

already been in Oxford for a few weeks. There was a coach, it ran twenty-four/seven, and she would go and stare at her old flat. She used to share it with some friends, but the lease ran out as she was leaving and they couldn't find a flatmate in time to be able to afford staying. Which was a shame – it was a nice place in Hammersmith. She would get off the bus around Shepherd's Bush and walk up the road she used to walk every day. It took her a while to get used to the idea that it wasn't hers any more. But once her new reality had set in, she went to see what the new tenants were doing in her old flat. They often left the curtains open, and from across the street, she could appraise all the decorating they'd done. Ghislane stopped looking at me and began musing over the place in her mind. Her face changed: they had made the flat *wrong*. They had put ugly little chairs in front of the fireplace where she had used to sit on rugs. They had stripped out the wallpaper, which had clearly been there from the seventies and smelt like it too. She couldn't blame them for that, but – she came out of her reverie and focused back on me – the flat's former derelict authenticity had been so aesthetically pleasing. Now it all looked brand new. They had convinced the landlord to let them do it up in cream and chrome. On a moral level she hated all of this, she sniffed, but on a material one, she felt deprived. The extent to which the whole road had been gentrified dawned on her just as she moved out. For most of her stay there, it had resembled something more like a construction site and so she had ignored its daily goings-on. This was no longer the case. Now that the transformation was complete, she resented the fact that other people got to enjoy a yoga studio and

19

coffee bar which she had only ever registered as a bombardment at her front door.

I tried to speak carefully. But her move notwithstanding, wasn't it probable they were gentrifying it for people like her?

Ghislane raised an eyebrow. You're swilling twenty pounds' worth of bubbly in that one glass alone, she intoned, and waited for a response. I didn't take the bait. She sighed, became, by degrees, visibly bored. I could see the boys who had accosted her earlier drawing in. Finally, she said, It was cheap when I moved in and Hammersmith reminded me of being at St Paul's. Do you have Instagram?

This threw me a little. I said I did. She seemed cheered.

Okay, sweet. Look, add me on that – she thrust her phone at me – we can talk some other time. I plugged my username onto the screen. She took it back and was gone. Things moved fluidly, as if staged. The boys arrived as she left, looking earnestly after her. The questions came thick and rapid. Was she leaving? What did she say? Did she say where she was going? Why had she given me her phone? When I told them she had asked me to add her on Instagram, the boys exchanged looks.

Fuck me, one of them said, no one said it was a networking event.

I was getting irate. They looked at me with pity, as if I were slow. You've never heard of her before, the other asked, have you?

I wanted to protest. I had just met her.

They snickered and walked away. Out of the corner of my eye I could see one remaining bottle of champagne on the drinks table to my right. I hadn't managed to speak to anyone else. The party could not be approached in any useful way. There were, at most, only four years separating me from the students in the room, and despite the seniority of my position, it was impossible not to feel inadequately young. It would not have surprised me if the boys who had asked after Ghislane had mistaken me for a classmate – I could not claim much on them except a minimum-wage job. We had too many higher powers in common: faculty lecturers; the student finance page of gov.uk. I looked around. I was too shy to approach anyone else. I moved towards the table of champagne, wrapped the last bottle inside my cardigan and slipped out.

The googling was swift, efficient. Thanks to her Instagram handle, I had her last name. Out on South Parks Road, the boys' scoffing began to make sense. She was not merely named after a song, it was her father who had sung it in the mid-nineties and it had made him a hit. There was a Wikipedia page: Ghislane's mother had also been called Ghislane. She had left them, hence the song. I had no headphones, but let it play. The sound quality was low and most of it went into the wind. It was just possible to make out the melody, whining melancholy and faux-folk. When it was done, I went back to Instagram. This was how I walked up the lamplit street. At the party I had only known Ghislane for fifteen minutes. Now, I had known her for five years. Our acquaintance fell in line with the upward momentum of my thumb. Here was Ghislane posing in front of the Bodleian in an announcement post for her temporary new home. There she was back in London, surrounded by faces I did not know. The span of her life took up as much space and time as the pixels and confines of my phone – it was like being at a museum. You walked in, everything was in galleries on show. Occasionally, you came up against barriers which stopped you from observing too closely, but for the most part, you looked freely where you liked, and decided whether or not you found it beautiful. Above all, you checked to see if other people found it beautiful too, a process by which what you were doing became less strange. Ghislane was not as famous as her father, but there were the beginnings of some distinction there, a small level of intrigue around who she was. The articles about her only extended as far back as the year, and came mostly through a slew of fashion websites which proclaimed that the last years of the decade would see a nineties revival. Pictures from her socials were set next to images of the song's music video and offered as proof. I reached the bottom of one of her feeds and moved on to the next.

The end of South Parks Road connected to a main one along the University Parks, running parallel to the city centre. If I'd walked ten minutes north, I would have hit the road back to my room. The champagne, still held awkwardly between some knit fabric and my torso, slipped every so often with the slouch of my spine as my face and my screen got increasingly closer. I stopped walking; stood still, scrolled until the phone stopped me, flashing symbols green and red for me to choose whether to receive a call. I waited impatiently for them to go away. Then a message came through.

Bored yet?

My neighbour met me on an alleyway off the High Street wearing white tie and dress shoes. With these, the cobblestones did him no favours. He hobbled over to me.

Well – there was an appraisal – you're a bit under-dressed.

I began to dislike him again.

I told him he hadn't said it would be white tie, but he rebuffed this quickly with an apology and the explanation that he thought it was evident: he had told me the event was a formal. You'll learn, he said. I told him this was unlikely, my contract was only nine months, but he beckoned me to follow anyway. I wanted to ask why on earth I would be expected to spend my evenings in white tie; why time spent in the company of ordinary people and alcohol should necessitate wearing a gown and arranging my hair, but without looking to see whether I'd fallen into step, he had already begun to lead the way. I had no choice but to follow.

We climbed several flights of stairs. He kept looking at me dubiously and murmuring things like, The dinner's already done…not even that bad a dress…yes…no…oh, bugger us, it's fine. He went ahead and through a series of complicated corridors, spouting reassurances all the way. I popped the cork on the champagne. He turned back at the sound and looked alarmed.

How did you know I wouldn't enjoy the department party? I asked, aggrieved.

Wisdom of the expert. This, over his shoulder. It's not that I knew *you* wouldn't like it, it's that I'm sure *I* don't like them.

I had known him for a day. If there was anything in me that found a reflection in him, I wanted to scrub myself clean of it. But I did not say this out loud. I took another hit of champagne and asked why that meant anything.

There are better ways to spend your time is what I meant, he said. He came to a halt in front of a door, frowned at my dress again, then opened it, gesturing half-heartedly that I should go inside.

I stayed where I was and glowered.

All right. He held up his hands and apologised. The formal's over anyway, this is just a drinks thing now. Are you trying to glower? It's very impressive. Come on, come in. I'm sure no one will mind.

In this way, I was ushered gently into a room full of people I did not want to meet. They were all immaculately groomed. Around them, the perimeter of the room was lined with portraits of men and women who, for some reason, regardless of the image's style, were only ever painted in old age. From the walls, everything within was watched unblinkingly.

I watched it, too, for a few minutes. I had not eaten. The champagne had begun to course through my head. I turned to my neighbour and said, I think I'm going to die in this room, which he ignored. There was no water in sight anywhere. I found a seat.

Things happened around me whether I acted in relation to them or not. Despite the Indian summer, the heating switched on automatically, heedless of the sweltering mass it induced. People threw open windows, slid ice into their drinks. Because there was only so much seating, they took to the floor, and because there was only so much floor, they migrated endlessly, roving in and out of my line of view. I found my phone and sent my neighbour a text.

Need water. Help.

I remained like this for a while until I heard my neighbour say – Here – reappearing at my side. He slipped the neck of the bottle of champagne deftly downwards out of my grip so that he could slide a glass of water back in. When I finished it, he smiled and handed the bottle back, asking whether I had met anyone. As he did, he waved a man over who introduced himself through thick-rimmed glasses and an Irish accent. When the pleasantries were done, the Irish man turned his back to me, apparently resuming a conversation he had been having with my neighbour before the latter had come to my rescue. From what I could tell, my neighbour had voted to leave, while his friend had voted to remain. They updated each other on what was ostensibly the same news cycle, but each with a different spin. As they went on, more people joined to have their say. I understood the necessity of my neighbour handing me my drink back. I gulped some more and closed my eyes. The conversation began to sound like broadcast radio, with belligerent callers dropping in. The voices said things like – the problem is, she wants to please everyone, and you can't make policy through those means – *yes*, but a *Canada*-style deal creates a border in the Irish Sea – *worst* PM for the job – why should the integrity of the United Kingdom be threatened by a tariff clause? – yes, but the doorstop – absolute shit-show, we're the laughing stock of the world – don't be an idiot, she was gagging for it, have you seen her record as Home Sec? – I voted for sovereignty, you can't have a country without that – change a decades-old arrangement at the drop of a hat and the change of a law – Chequers was always going to be a non-starter – it's what you get when you put a geography degree in office, to be honest – did you say *doorstop*? It's *backstop*, you silly cunt – feel sorry for her – don't even want to be part of this country any more, I got an Irish passport done – clearly don't even know what you mean when you say it, so why butt in? You're just regurgitating what you read – yes, me too, impossible task, but when you think about those *vans* she sent round – okay, Dr Google, tell me: what is a backstop, then? –

I opened one bleary eye and found my phone still in my hand. I sent my neighbour the same text again – *Need water. Help.* I watched him start at the buzz of his phone, then roll his eyes. Just a second, he told his friends. He picked his way over, and then he hung above me, studying my face with a barely repressed laugh.

Home time? He grinned. I wanted a brilliant remark to cut him down with but forming distinct sentences was hard. At last, I managed to slur, Why'd you give me more champagne for?

Terrible grammar for a lit grad, he observed, then heaved me up from the side. I hit his back as best I could, then allowed myself to be led from the room. On our way out, he waved to the friend he had introduced me to and said, Round two over dinner. To which his friend – In that kitchen? Like fuck. You're coming to me.

Bit pointless worrying about the dress code, I said once we had cleared the door. Everyone ended up taking off their clothes anyway. You've all ended up more undressed than me. And another thing, I gasped once we had passed the corridor, I don't understand. None of your friends are English. All their voices sounded European. Except for your Irish mate – he was Irish.

He said, Yep, and began hauling me down the stairs. I snorted. Does that make it difficult to look them in the eye? I asked. Did you know them when you voted Leave? It's funny how no one around here is actually from here, isn't it?

My neighbour sighed. I can be friends with them and disagree, he said.

I don't think you can be friends with people you voted to boot out of the country they've made their home in, mate, I informed him. He began to hold me at arm's length with no answer. I mean, I pressed on, did you see the images they used for the Leave campaign? Are you a racist?

At this, he pulled me in very close, until I could see him directly in spite of the champagne. He looked appalled. I voted for stronger laws around our borders, he said. I voted for sovereignty. It's as black and white as that. He let me go. I drew myself together without his help as best I could.

Well, *excuse* me, I exhaled, but a party is only a good one if you invite other people in, you know? I thought I was being deeply philosophical. I was quite drunk. I nodded several times and waited for him to absorb the depth of my statement. He left me at the bottom of the stairs.

I.V.i

The academic year had not fully started. Term was not due for another two weeks. Parties left their mark on the city centre. In the mornings, there was glitter wedged between the cobblestones; cans of beer placed politely on top of public rubbish bins. There was a McDonald's on Cornmarket Street: it played Vivaldi to the under-graduates slumped sideways at 5 a.m., waiting for a Happy Meal to take back to their rooms. Outside it, concrete slabs of benches were divided with sharp metal rails. The last of September slipped into October but the heat held time still. Halloween displays remained stacked full with decorations and chocolate next to near-empty coolers of ice cream – in the evenings, I ripped a share bag of candy off one, and fished a Cornetto out of the other: dinner. I queued for self-checkout machines and blended in with lines of students clutching tins of chopped tomatoes and sliced bread.

And when the next opportunity to do so came, I delivered an apology to my neighbour. I said, I'm sorry for asking whether you're a racist, and after a while he managed a smile and said, Ah well, I suppose it's always better to check. But some awkwardness still cast its pall, so I asked, Who else lives here? and invited him in for a conciliatory cup of tea. He didn't speak to them, but there were five other tenants in separate rooms, and below us, a couple in the converted basement flat. Some of them had been there as long as him. He could hear them when the floorboards squeaked or the doors slammed, or when the smell of the coffee they had brewed seeped around the adjoining rooms. I began to recognise them this way, too. I listened for creaks on the landing when I came out of the shower to make sure the hall was clear, tiptoed the corridor back to my room, trailing droplets of hastily rinsed shampoo. Quickly, I discerned nuances in tread and gradually an association between them and different smells from the communal kitchen: heavy tread, mango curry; skittish run, boiled rice; soft, slow step, garlic and chicken. When each set of footsteps retreated back into its room, I crept down to inspect the leftover crumbs and tea towels, and dishes piled like stained white ghosts in the sink.

Nothing happened. I tried to watch the news with my neighbour, but often found I couldn't. He laughed at it, which horrified me. I watched reruns of *Friends* instead and resented the fact that Monica never asked any of the characters for rent, even when she worked a waitress job in a diner, even when she couldn't get a catering job for four months. I listened to the laugh track echo around her purple and chintz living room: dull, soothing mono-glossia. The arc of the Friends' lives changed, but the times never did. Characters got better jobs, got married, upgraded the apartment and left for better housing, and the laugh track stayed the same – was that meliorism?

I wondered. No presidents got impeached, twin towers did not fall. New Yorkers walked around the city, unheeding of bomb plots, or terror, or war. If the show had managed to trundle on long enough for the markets to crash, would Chandler have lost his job? Perhaps Ross might have left his lectureship and museum in the wake of the budget cuts to education. But would I have wanted to watch that? What else did anyone with comfortable enough means ever really do, except look at the news and accept the circumstances of the world so long as they did not interfere with the general course of what it took to live a life? I watched it as it was and did nothing, turning screens on and off in my room.

But on the seventh day, there was a knock on my door, and a woman in a hoodie and pinafore peered into my room. She said, Rubbish? Clean? She had a face gently carved with freckles and lines; a coil of greying brown hair. Her English rolled and lisped. Spanish? I asked. She shook her head. *Maria*, she corrected. Maria came in and began to unburden me of any simple responsibility I might have had in that room. And when she made to spray cleaning fluid on the sink, when she took out rags for the bookshelves' dust, when she plugged the Hoover in and set the brush to roll and suck along the floor, my cowardice overtook me. I left for a walk.

Outside, I found Ghislane leaning back from the house, taking in the Paters' plaque with her phone's camera lens. It was perhaps her absorption in this task, perhaps the hedge that obscured my coming out, which meant she did not see me. I approached her from the side and made my best attempt. I said, Are you looking for me? But she seemed confused. It was never what I thought. Her eye roved and shuttered. She took the measure of the light, angled, cut and framed. Finally, instead – I'm writing on aestheticism – and – Why are you here? – and – I wonder what they do with this place now. I shrugged. She began to talk about how incredible it was, Pater having a plaque when all his life he was deemed a vacuous and immoral pleasure-seeker on account of his being gay. I made to talk as well, but her phone buzzed, and she was away.

A beat. I stood. I checked Instagram. Ghislane's account. And there, already, a selfie in front of the house (swipe) a closer crop on the plaque (scroll down) Pater quoted below the post overall. *The impress of a personal quality, a profound expressiveness, what the French call intimité, by which is meant a subtler sense of originality, the seal on a man's work of what is most inward and peculiar in his moods and manner of apprehension: it is what we call expression carried to its highest intensity of degree.*

The top of Ghislane's head in the selfie blocked out a stain of bird shit on one of the first-floor windows. I looked at the window itself, less spectacular than what I had just seen on my phone. The brickwork was less defined; lighter. I looked back at my screen – she was radiant around it, and it looked better. When the house belonged to her, it was a magnificent thing. I resumed my walk.

At the end of Broad Street, the petal-pink pub; its dark wood interior; the overspill of future ministers onto the pavement, past its doors; and there, visible, their uncertainty, their apprehension towards a girl holding an India pale, paid for with her government loan. (I walked.)

31

Past the pub, Wren's rotunda. Its duck-egg-blue dome. The curve of a hall. The Bodleian's castle of books adjoining. In both, the turnover of robed crows graduating; in both, their black wings flapping; in both, the echo of what they swear fealty to. That centuries-old chant, *Do fidem*, binding them to what they've learned. Underneath, the same boys with a difficult relationship to what predicate a subject may reasonably perform within its clause. Boys who believe in teddy bears and plovers' eggs as a political cause. On the wind, their performance; the ceremonials, the Latin few of them know. (I walked.) *Do fidem* to that ceiling of angels painted centuries ago. It all ascends: *the admirable smoke and drink and the deep armchairs and the pleasant carpets: the urbanity, the geniality, the dignity which are the offspring of luxury and privacy and space.* Three years spent having dinner delivered from an invisible kitchen to a well-adorned hall. A degree in pursuit of public service while white gloves put out plates of slow-cooked duck with an orange-and-ginger sauce. (I walked.) *Do fidem*, out they come. Picture them polishing shoes and a CV. The bridge sighs. What would there be to make them, if not where they came from? *Intellectual freedom depends on material things.* Everywhere, the heavy wooden doors and keyhole's false promise. Everywhere, the push and pull of magnet strips, the binary code: a database and no chance of entry so random as finding a piece of metal to turn in a hole. (I walked.) Everywhere, languor. *Do fidem.* What keeps it pretty? *Do fidem.* At what point does intention evolve?

*

At Turl Street, I stopped for coffee and imagined Maria letting herself into the other tenants' rooms. She removed spit and toothpaste from sinks, she lifted hair from carpets, she opened windows and let fresh air overtake all other smells. She unhooked her master key from her belt and made steady progress; knew the house as a whole to be able to clean out any trace of us having been there.

Now put it this way: not they, but you. *Once, presumably, this quadrangle with its smooth lawns, its massive buildings and the chapel itself was marsh too: teams of horses and oxen must have hauled the stone in wagons from far countries and then with infinite labour the grey blocks were poised in order. Oxbridge is an invention; 'I' is only a convenient term for somebody who has no real being.* How much can be composed from guilt, and the place that you are in? Infinite amounts and nothing at all. (As I walked, I scrolled.) Points won: there is the gravel, you are a woman, you are brown, you have made it here. Points lost: there is the turf, you were born bourgeois in your comforts and desires. Now see them both and decide which is true. When you lean into one, you watch the other rescinded. *Nil pwa*, the twenty-first century's great game is to collapse all of history into a pixel; an impression; a now. Who are you then? (I scrolled.) You are brown and bourgeois, and the internet does not believe you exist. You believe in equal opportunity and the welfare state. You believe in home-ownership and a competitive CV. Riot or march, all it comes down to is neoliberal shame. Points won: a sandwich and change to the man in blankets in front of the college stone. Points lost: the stone has an entryway, the pass to which you own. The common room, the carpet, the armchairs: you know, in no small way, the privilege of a place can depend on the absence of the wrong body as much as the presence of the right one. It is not impossible to shift the relationship between tradition and what is strange. Now you are inside, and does it occur to you to ask him in? *Do fidem: no need to hurry. No need to sparkle. No need to be anything but oneself.*

(I scrolled.)

Once I felt I had walked for long enough I turned back. The room was clean and Maria was gone. I ran the tap for a few moments. I upset a pillow. I trekked grass and dirt from my shoes into the carpet, sprayed some perfume in the air and threw my coat on an easy chair. Ghislane's post itched at the back of my skull and, because of it, a well-worn line. *To see the object as in itself it really is, is to know one's own impression as it really is, to discriminate it, to realise it distinctly.*

I had always thought Pater was ahead of his time. The book that sentence had come from, *The Renaissance*, practically foresaw Instagram, with its insistence on dogged individualism as a mode of perception, its insistence on personal aesthetics as vision and feeling. I took my copy down from the room's shelves; began walking in circles with it in one hand and Ghislane's Instagram account on my phone in the other. Only two weeks had passed since I had last looked properly at her account, and still she had managed to fill her immediate grid with unfamiliar posts. I scrolled through what I had not yet seen and tried to find a Pater quote to ascribe to each one.

34

First turn around the room. Pater argued that for something to have true value – value which could touch and alter the soul – its maker would have to transcend the conventions of their era through the absolute expression of their own temper and personality. That which was unique and utterly subjective to one's self in the context of set environments, in other words, a good amount of egoism, was the source of beauty and worth. And there Ghislane was: wearing subfusc and utterly herself in the middle of a thirteenth-century college hall and portraits of distinguished alumni surrounding her on every wall. When her make-up was perfectly done. How she held a tiny, striped Mansur Gavriel with both hands. The entire set-up was so immaculate I came to a halt. This was not the absolute expression of her. Who enshrined her onscreen as though they did not exist? I knew they were there, holding the phone. Could I pull my thumbs in opposite directions widely enough across the screen; zoom to check whether their reflection could be found in those aged luminaries, instructing her pose. Would the oil paint be shiny enough for that. I looked for Ghislane's caption – *giving the company some spice* – and found it was Paterian enough.

Second turn around the room. Now who Ghislane was. Now a gold quilted throw on the bed. A hook, dangling beads off the wall; the drawn curtains, decanted whiskey and Dove deodorant aerosol. The box of Weetabix and the used bowl, and the Anne Carson on the shelves; the paper on the desk and the pen angled neatly, just so. The staged authenticity of the room. Ghislane called it, *My true messy self*. And of course, Pater likewise agreed that one could *accomplish their*

*function in the choice and development of some special
situation, which lifts or glorifies a character in itself not
poetical. To realise this situation, the artist has to employ
the most cunning detail, to complicate and refine upon
thought and passion a thousand-fold.* I assessed the
cunning detail of my own space and found it not poetical enough. I took my coat from the easy chair and put
it on a hanger. I lit a candle. I fussed my duvet until I
felt better. I began to take my third turn around the
room, but knocked my knee on the corner of my desk
and found myself dizzy. I sat on the floor to judge the
succeeding photo as the last.

Ghislane well knew what an event was when it
occurred and stood with admirable readiness to arrest it.
It could be anything. Such as: *my girls.* So – an event
was several girls clasped to each other on Ashmolean
stairs, becoming caryatids in neon tops and Topshop
jeans. The tops of their heads crested the username in
her header. They held it up. They were attentive to the
shutter of the lens. And Ghislane was aware, there was
no doubt in my mind she was aware, that in documenting
this she had created *a new sort of mythology with a tone
and qualities of its own.* Pater supposed that *when the
ship-load of sacred earth from the soil of Jerusalem was
mingled with the common clay in the Campo Santo at
Pisa, a new flower grew up from it.* I looked at the girls
immortalised laughing on the museum's mouldering
steps. The bloom of their camisoles and the stalks of
their legs. Because of Ghislane's phone, they would
always be there.

*

Not the fruit of experience, but experience itself is the end. To burn always with this hard gem-like flame, to maintain this ecstasy, is success in life. Failure is to form habits; for habit is relative to a stereotyped world. I laid myself out on the floor; contemplated the ceiling and allowed myself to be pissed off. Even Pater had made his impressions in a permanent room. Here I was, having walked circles in it, looking at Ghislane, who, with her song of a name, could dispense herself anywhere there was a radio or a phone.

I lay on the floor until I heard a knock; stiffened – but it was my neighbour, nudging the door open with his shoulder until I tipped my chin. I watched, critically, his big strides in. He gave me a once-over and concluded, Tea?

I raised myself up on my elbows and shot back, Do you ever drink anything else? Could we do orange juice, just to mix it up?

He put the kettle on anyway. *The Renaissance* fell into his line of sight as he did and he picked it up.

So this is the Pater chap.

Mmm.

Lovely of you to take the time. Go on. I still want to know all about him.

I went back down on the floor and mumbled, It wasn't for you, I was trying to see something.

He didn't take offence. I told him what it was I had been doing, and he finished making the tea. He placed a cup delicately by my side; stretched himself out next to me on the floor, balancing his in both hands on his stomach. Finally, he said, I don't get it. I looked at him, and he went on – You're the one who sleeps here, not

37

her. Pater's long-dead. What difference does it make who lived in this house before?

Well – I looked back up at the ceiling – that blue plaque outside probably added an extra hundred quid to our rent for a start.

I'm pretty sure the university did that.

I went on as though I had not heard. Ghislane seems to have found a new way to impress herself on a space that doesn't just rely on the physical. She filters herself into places via Instagram. The photos she puts up are perfectly posed; they're an overall representation of her taste and personality laid onto a profile that works as an overall microcosm of her*self*. And it works so well, she can do it with anything, even with photos of settings which clearly don't belong to her. Our house, for example. She uploaded this ridiculous photo where you can see her looking beautiful and quoting Pater in front of it, so it looks like she's far more familiar with it than she really is. See? I thrust my phone at him until he put his tea down and accepted it. We lay side by side. He had his arm in the air and Ghislane's Instagram hovering above us. He squinted at the grey glow of assorted pixels.

Impress herself on a space, my neighbour repeated with deliberate slowness. So because she took a picture of the house, she now lives here? Should I be cutting her a key?

Listen – I went up on my elbows again and made sure he could see the irritation on my face. Take your bastard tea and get out. But he took this as a joke. Okay, he said when he'd finished laughing, in the first place, it's your tea we're drinking, but let's say what you're proposing does matter. Clearly you've got a nice grip on how important Pater is to this place. So you're fine, no? Take a photo of the house. I'll be the first to congratulate you on living here, too.

I grabbed my phone; went to sit up properly out of frustration, but in so doing knocked over the mug he had placed next to me. I scrambled; ran to the toilet for tissues. When I got back, I found him just the same, watching the stain soak into the carpet.

For fuck's sake, I snapped, and shooed him away so that I could clean the mess. He laughed again. Look, you're already ruining the place, he said. It's definitely yours now.

The tissues kept disintegrating before they could properly soak up the tea. I gave up using them and fished the T-shirt of my pyjama set from out under my pillow. I was on my knees and he was stood two paces away, watching me attend to the patches of umber blossoming from out of the carpet into my clothes. It's not mine, I said. It's not mine because I don't know how to do the thing Ghislane does. And now I'm going to have to pay for this stain out of my deposit. And you've made me ruin my fucking pyjamas.

I looked up at him. He sighed. It's okay, he said. I get it. The limbo between terms gets me a bit funny as well.

I.V.ii

On the eighth of October I set an alarm that went off at 5.45 a.m. the next day with a sharp peal. It split me from my bed. I saw the room come into light with the first article Twitter hyperlinked onto my screen and learned that workers' rights were to be diminished *even in the event of a deal*. This article proposed the creation of a common rulebook of rights, breaches of which could be dealt with by a supranational court. This article proposed that the deregulation of workers' rights was an opportunity for the UK to match, if not surpass, other nations in the creation of new ones. This article failed to tell me what my soon-to-be stripped rights were, and so it was impossible to worry in a way that wasn't vague. It was hard to feel specifically outraged. In any event, the establishment of a supranational court was a far more interesting theory to mull over because it seemed to me, as I lay in bed and philosophised in the aftershock of my alarm, that no one was above borders or nation, or some kind of entity they carried with them in lieu of home. A judge still had a passport, paid tax, at some point returned to a house plotted upon a piece of land.

I finished, pushed, with the upward swipe of my thumb, the article away and put the radio on; I spooned coffee grounds into a cafetière.

When it was done, the sound of an ironically titled daily bird programme on Radio 4, *Tweet of the Day*, swam back into the room: a voice like sandpaper soothing wood into a level plane reported not on sound as news, but on sound as natural phenomena. It told me I was listening to larks' songs recorded from Spain. I pressed the plunger down on my cafetière and felt idyllic. Five short tones and a final long one signalled the beginning of the *Today* programme and set me back to work. A plummy rich voice warbled in and out of focus, and on each hour, the Greenwich Time Signal carved the occasions of that morning into distinct parts. To them, teeth cleaned, a hot towel passed over pores, rolled nylon flat over thighs. I transposed the room into a bag. House key, fob, vanity mirror, shawl, tissues, set text, lanyard, Vaseline Lip Therapy, a sheaf of notes. I left the house and listened to it all rattle under my arm.

Ghislane did not appear in the Bodleian, the English faculty library, nor its dark wood and glassy building. Over the course of a few weeks, I recognised those students she had pointed out at the department party, who now seemed like pale creations without her estimations of them, given over a glass of champagne and driving them on. Eventually I tamed the little impulse that asked where she was. Then, for a while, things became the same. The days shortened. Dust fell on routine. I transcribed manuscripts and learned how not to fall asleep in front of online databases. I ate shop-bought vegan wraps with bad chipotle and an abundance of starch. I kept spare change for coffee. In the morning, the wake-up radio beat out pips of time before the same road, the same load under my arm as I went – eventually I could have done it in my sleep. Eastbound path through the park towards the faculty. Four hours later, down Holywell Street, until I hit Broad Street. And the papers to look over. And lectures to sit in on, then hear translated in another seminar. I stopped craving candy for dinner. Only the fire drills carried out by the college accommodation office disturbed the peace: irregularly done and with the siren, occasionally, an accompanying knock on the door, at which point the house was timed for the efficiency of its evacuation. It was the only time I ever saw tenants other than my neighbour – once a month, with sleep in their eyes, in boxer shorts or slogan T-shirts and their arms wrapped around their chests for warmth, averting their gaze from each other's pyjamas.

When October was done, November ceased to exist. Shop windows dressed to look like living rooms with a centrepiece tree and wrapped presents underneath obscured time's flow. On walks home, I kept to the shade around Christmas lights which cast their glow over street markets selling hot chocolate to passers-by. Gingerbread men and thick woollen socks affected cosiness. To all this, I expected snow, which did not come, but frost set over the building's roofs and windowpanes: the city, beatified, and tourists in ill-suited shoes, trying not to skid.

I worked. Between seminars and on my lunch breaks I became obsessed with an oil painting by Turner, hung landscape in the Ashmolean. It was dated 1810 and showed the High Street, looking west: University College on the frame's left and the spire of St Mary's rising above everything. Each cobblestone and window was exact. I took a photo of the canvas and carried it to the High Street – held my phone up so that the beadles, the scholars in their gowns, were suddenly thrust into present day. Then I took a photo of the High Street as I knew it and held it up to the canvas the next time I saw it; lined it up so that it filled the painting's frame. I went back, from week to week, holding up photos with varying lights, kinds of weather, shifting casts. I considered asking my neighbour whether he would take a picture of me on the High Street so that I could later crop the photo and insert myself into Oxford, 1810 – but embarrassment prevented me from doing so. I did not want to be thought of as sad, or vain.

I worked. I had disputes with my supervisor on his students' tutorial essays. He took these lightly; I did not. He laughed good-naturedly over a paper on archive and the environment, and what to do with all the world's paper once climate change brought us down to bare necessities. It said: eat the rich for fuel; vote which litera-ture goes into bunkers by popular rule. I argued strongly for one he disliked on the difference between what the American literary domestic was and the UK's notion of home. In America, everyone was always searching for home. Who could lay claim? Huck Finn and Jim floating four walls on a raft down the river, picking up grifters as they went; Nick Carraway marvelling at the summer bungalow he was newly able to rent. America's foremost piece of literature was its Constitution, which tied its politics inextricably to its land – the question of who owned it, and who had tilled it; the disparity between the two. In England, only myths, only fictions defined the land: Chaucer's pilgrims and their tales; Wordsworth, spinning his prophecy to open vales. In England, there was no question of home: depending on who you were, it was either always there, or not. It all worked by empire, by assumption. An orphan girl could advertise and inherit another woman's burnt trove. Orlando found nothing different within themself in the same mirror, hung within the same ancestral abode. The rest went unmentioned. I emailed him to say I thought this deserved high praise. I'm uneasy about essays which come down strongly on one side, he replied. Few essays make such expansive arguments with rigour. Dialectics create more intelligent arguments: ideas are better served when they are complicated rather than cheered or booed as at a football match. I replied, of course, and stared, suddenly deflated, at the screen.

I worked. I found a girl Ghislane had pointed out to me at the party crying quietly in a Starbucks on Cornmarket – burnout, anxiety, SAD. I asked if she was all right.

The country's going to hell and I can't finish my essay, she said. How do I know what matters when I can't get a look-in? Marking criteria were too vague, and, besides, didn't I know? May was holding private meetings with backbench MPs. The pound hit a twenty-month low – what use was an English degree now that fake news had eliminated the meaning of words anyway? The vote was delayed, the tick on her word count wouldn't grow.

There was general bewilderment that it should all be going this slow. She crumpled in her chair – I just *feel* I've fallen behind on my personal self-care.

Relax, I said. Keep yourself healthy. Take long walks. Take a bath with oils. Find a Boots and take Bach Rescue Remedy. Perhaps it should have occurred to me to say, Take responsibility for the degree you paid for and chose, but before I thought to, confidence was partially restored. After she left, the words hung uselessly in the air.

I worked. In the evenings, my neighbour interrupted me with news updates and jasmine tea: he had a new girlfriend, or so he thought. She was Czech, he couldn't quite tell. He was sleeping with her, but he couldn't quite tell – what was the deal with women now? When she said things, he was convinced there was subtext, but every time he asked her for it, she looked at him confused, and made him feel mad. I soaked my mouth in warm, fragrant water which absolved me of the expectation of response – he was free to talk on end. He wasn't on Twitter, he said, and real time didn't seem to be a fast-enough pace to keep up with changing social codes. Should he open doors for her? Should he take it for granted that she would come and go? Should he text her, and ask her to let him know? Even the waiters didn't know which way the bill should go if they went out for lunch. One time, the thin white strip tucked discreetly into leather was waved back and forth over them, as though their server sensed this was not yet a relationship of equals and equilibrium. In the end, it was decided he should pay for rented use of knives and forks, of linen, now stained with overcooked pork. And she, my neighbour groaned, half smiled, half bristled, as though it were ludicrous that he should pay, but he may as well now, all the same. It was the most confusing and expensive relationship he had ever known, and yet he was a willing participant in its misery.

I worked. I went to an advisory session on mental health and well-being. The world was a difficult place, the internet even more so. I had found the equivalent of a lonely hearts column in Oxford, a Facebook page called Oxlove, and another for the airing of grievances, Oxfess, and wasted hours a day going through them. *Why is every girl here a basic white girl??? Even the brown ones*; and *beret man, feel free to chirpse on Monday, will be wearing silver boots* (below, tagged, a number of men pictured in berets and *omg is this you?*); and *definitive ranking of Christmas sandwiches, if u rate the M&S one, ur a Tory*; and *To the incredibly kind girls who picked me up off the floor on Bridge Thursday, you've restored my faith in humanity*; and *TRIGGER WARNING MENTAL HEALTH – I just don't see any point in going on*; and *we live in a society*; and *zero-hour contracts and low wage is pretty much the norm, last week I saw the homeless guy outside college disappear and no one noticed*; and *ugh, can someone explain why middle class is a dirty word, like it's my *fault**; and, *y'all will like memes about having zero in your bank account and then go back to the Home Counties to your five-bedroomed house owned outright by your parents, I hate you all, y'all have no idea what it's actually like to struggle*. Stay off the internet, the mental health adviser advised.

I worked. My mother kept interrupting to tell me I never called; to tell me I never came home; to ask whether I wanted to join her and my father on holiday for a month. I told her I could not take that kind of time off work, and I was still settling in. I needed that month to make my new life stable, but would wait and see whether I could go home for a week sometime soon. She told me I'd go into an early grave. I said, well, that's how it was these days, and subsequently received a chain of WhatsApp messages. This was not what she expected from any daughter of hers; could I not just take the damn holiday, it's not like I would even have to pay for it; why could I not at least pretend to be grateful, and by the way, this was my father's view on the matter, too. We did not speak over Christmas. When she got back in touch to tell me they had returned to the country safely, something had changed. She asked me about my life in the same forced, dutiful tone of voice I used to ask about her trip.

I worked. In the literary journals I researched in, advertising overtook articles and declared property for sale. *Escape from Brexit for the tranquillity of rural Ireland. A book lover's home with shelving and a study. Two adjacent traditional cottages in County Clare, sleeping five, plus seven acres, but handy for Shannon airport and the wild Atlantic coast, for €285,000 or equivalent.* Below that: *Calm German writer looking for a room in New York City. My novel caused a scandal in Germany. NYC is my exile.*

And in the New Year, there was a TV film – *Brexit*, with bad wigs and a dramatic score. It was criticised by those who watched it from a streaming service offered by Channel 4. The events of 2016 played out over again. Twitter became a country divided. The times were already a costume drama. You could get used to anything if it was administered in the correct dose.

I began to have strange dreams over this period. The news bled into them. Perhaps it was a natural side effect of listening to the radio first thing in the morning and reading my Twitter feed at night – but they were disappointingly sedate. In one of them, I met an amalgam politician, a composite of centrist, start-of-the-decade neoconservative ideals, and he was not so unreasonable that I felt I could decline his invitation to breakfast. He led me with overblown courteousness to the hall of his former college, where we settled on a bench in the middle of the room. You sit, and I'll choose for you, he grinned, and bounded off. He returned with two trays laden with small pots of Bonne Maman jam, boiled eggs, butter, bacon, then held a finger up and disappeared once more. When he came back, it was with a rack of toast and a coffee pot. He took his phone out of his pocket and placed it, screen up, on the table. I imitated him. Finally, he sat down.

Now, then – he surveyed me over the table – you look like…those, I think. He pushed two of the small pots of raspberry conserve towards me. He buttered me a piece of toast and set it down on my plate, where it went ignored. He didn't seem to notice or mind. Having done his due diligence towards me, he piled his plate with bacon and began cutting up another square of toast into thin slices with gusto. When this was done he took another plate, set his knife above it and sliced the head

48

off of an egg. Yolk slopped up from over the rim of the shell. The mess took thirty seconds to make. I poured myself a cup of coffee. I asked the burning question my dream self apparently wanted to know.

What was boarding school like?

The politician shot me a pained glance through a mouthful of bacon. Hell, if you must know, he said. I willed him to say more. He began to look like he rather regretted inviting me into the hall. It was boring, he said finally. It was school.

It was just a boring school? I sounded incredulous to myself even in my dream, as though the investment of my subconscious time was yielding conspicuously low return.

Yes, he said. In spite of himself, he stopped chewing momentarily and seemed to catch the end of a stray thought. It occurred to me later this could not have been the case given that all reality as it took place in that hall was constructed entirely out of my own. In any case, the politician swallowed his bacon, more of which had somehow multiplied on the plate before him, and said, I tell you what though, the night parties were fun.

There came a martyred sigh to indicate he didn't need prompting any more. A few more eggs had begun to rock on their sides on the plate in front of him, sloughing their shells. I went to eat my toast, but it had disappeared.

You got split into houses, where you got given your own room, he explained. Then you got a timetable. Regimented sort of thing: eat then, sleep then, shit then, lessons in between. I imagine it was meant to inspire a sense of discipline but obviously the only thing a curfew could inspire was the urge to break it. We'd sneak bottles of anything we could into each other's rooms at night and one-up each other.

What, I asked, 'I've seen more naked girls than you have'?

Don't be crass. Yes. But also, my god is better than your god kind of thing. It was intellectual, too.

I snorted, and he shot me a dirty look. Don't laugh, he said. You could really make or break yourself on these things. I remember one night, there was this boy, Felix, who almost ruined me. He began to slice up another piece of toast. The eggs he had been eating, meanwhile, had disappeared from his plate and reappeared on mine. He transferred them back onto his. Then he continued. It was my first night party. I had sherry that I'd stolen from my mother's pantry because I'd just been home for the weekend, and I invited the whole bloody house into my tiny room.

And?

It went great. I was the toast of the town, as it were. He looked at his buttered soldiers and chortled. Anyway, we had a good night, but of course, at some point they all had to go back to their own rooms, otherwise the dame—

The *what*?

Like a matron, he sped on impatiently, she would have had kittens. We all got caught at one point or another, actually, it's not easy to make it back to your dorm when you're drunk.

I opened my mouth to express my condolences but he shot me a warning look and I shut up. I took some toast from the rack; the butter, the jam; began making myself breakfast. He selected another egg with exaggerated solemnity.

There I am, trying to get them all out of my room, and the last person left is Felix, who pipes up and says, I feel terribly ill. May I sleep here? And because the party had been such a success, and I was feeling magnanimous the way you do when you're sixteen, I said yes. But only if he slept on the floor, cleared off in the morning and didn't tell anyone about it. Instead, I woke up at three in the morning to find him next to me in bed with a cramp in his leg from all the alcohol, making the most awful sort of noise—

What noise?

His plate was now a mountain of bacon. He pushed it aside to allow us a good view of each other, then screwed up his nose and closed his eyes. He began to moan in soft, vowel sounds. *Ai, ai, ai.* Awful noise, he said, face relaxed and eyes back open. I hated it. He kept holding his leg really tightly and making it worse. I ought to have hit him. The politician intuited my expression and rearranged his features accordingly. Yes, I know. I didn't, of course. Gave him some water, told him he'd be all right. He ran off anyway and I went back to bed. I didn't think any more of it, except he'd gone to the school nurse because he thought he was dying and the whole school found out that he'd stayed in my bed and had taken ill for an entire day after. The next morning I went down to breakfast. We ate in a hall with benches and the food was always cold – rather like this. He gestured vaguely at our surroundings within the college, the mess on his plates. Anyway, I sat down with my soldiers and my friends, and they're all congratulating

51

me on the night, and then someone yells quite loudly, *Apparently Felix got sick from sleeping in your bed.*

He paused. I had to quash all kinds of Chinese whispers after that. It sounds so odd to say, but this was years ago. Calling someone gay was still a credible insult. *Catching germs* from someone was still a viable notion. The UK and US hadn't even legalised same-sex marriage at that point.

We fell silent.

Actually, he resumed sheepishly, when I say he almost 'ruined' me, that might have been too grand a word.

I could think of nothing to say. He watched my face with ill-concealed anxiety, toying with some of the toast I'd made myself before tearing it, inattentively, into small pieces. At last, he could stand it no longer.

I've got nothing against people being gay, you know.

All right, I said. The politician paled. He said, I've got nothing against people being black, or brown, or them belonging to any kind of ethnic minority; nothing against them being gay, or bi, or trans; I have disabled friends, I support women's rights. I just couldn't let there be any confusion about Felix and my bed.

Oh. I shrugged. He nodded, satisfied, before springing forward again. I say, he smiled, would you mind making me some toast?

I stood up to fetch more bread and another plate. The dream morphed into something else.

When I woke up, what seemed strange to me was the fact that I had had no instinctive understanding of what this figure wanted or meant. Despite its presence in my subconscious, that apparent signal of my desire, if not design of its being there, I had not been able to find any veracity in its words, or feel any kinship with them as they came out. I knew only with certainty that I had been hungry, and that I had observed the ease with which sitting in that hall, piling up a plate, eating one's fill and telling a good story came to him. It was an unappealing characteristic, but not one I could truly say I had no sympathy with.

I.IV

When the snow came, it was late January and the park smelt of firs – it was reviving. I idled by the University Park gates, only a few minutes away from the house, in the evergreen air. Time to walk through them seemed to stretch into eternity, to be repeated again the following morning. I had taken to walking through the park on weekends, too. In lieu of work as destination, I crossed the high bridge that arched over the Cherwell. Behind it lay a sequence of farms and woodland, which I walked through. I used *Tweet of the Day* to pick out various birdsong, playing each two-minute segment through earphones at intervals. I got used to the smell of cowpat; knew at which time of day the sun would strike the grass gold. But a thin layer of frost and snow falling that morning in fat flurrying flakes turned the footpath slipshod. I went back, stripped off in my room save for knickers and a long sweater; went downstairs.

In the kitchen, the bins were overflowing. My neighbour greeted me from the table, but had tucked himself too tightly in with his chair and was unable to move.

He rolled his head around on his neck and watched my progress towards the rubbish.

Oh yeah. He gave a nod. I think Maria is on holiday.

I thought of Maria scrubbing his daily meal of baked beans and pasta off the kitchen countertops and hob, where it invariably reappeared the next afternoon. It was only the surplus of trash bulging from the bins that announced her absence. I tried not to feel shame, then reflected that perhaps doing so might make me a better person, and had a brief communion with it. When I was done, I looked around the kitchen. It was true, there was more tomato sauce splashed around than usual. I moved away from the countertops and bins and found the assembly of brightly coloured microfibre rags she left on the radiator each day to dry after she'd used them.

Oh, those are Maria's, my neighbour ventured uncertainly having watched me wet one and scrub the counter.

I'm aware, I said.

He bit his lip. I'm not sure we're supposed to touch them.

I could have hit him, but I didn't. I picked a dried baked bean off the hob, finished scrubbing and wiped the whole thing down. When the rag was replaced on the radiator alongside the others, I lifted the top off the bin and began to twist what corners I could grab of the rubbish bag in on themselves, then marched towards the front door in search of the neighbourhood wheelie bins. He watched on in anxious silence, breaking it only with the offer of a cup of tea.

I had already forgotten about the snow. I stuffed my feet into slippers. Outside, each little press of cold reminded me of the fact that I was wearing only a large jumper and a pair of knickers. An industrial waste container peeked visibly over the hedges surrounding the front of the house.

Not visible over the hedges and standing next to the bins was a boyish-looking man passing the house in a pink scarf and corduroy trousers. I halted before him, looked at the bag in my hand, and the goosetrail rising up my thighs. He in turn, with some bemusement, lifted the lid of the waste container up for me and watched as I heaved the bag in with one hand, and pulled the hem of my jumper down with the other. He replaced it leisurely when I was done, took a pocket hanky out of his shirt, and began gently wiping his fingers. He offered a smile.

I pulled my jumper down still further. He flicked his eyes downward and said, Oh, do stop worrying about *that*, it's nothing we haven't both seen before, which I didn't know whether to take as an insult or a sign of decency. It seemed easier to go for the latter and more correct to side with the former. I thanked him for his help and watched him walk on unperturbed.

All winter, I had been sitting in pubs and bars, waiting for someone to come over. Now, it was spring, and all I had was a declining rate on my debit card. April. I had ordered negronis. I had ordered Guinness on tap. I had held glasses of house white and whiskey in heavy-bottomed tumblers; downed little shots of coffee liqueur. A veil of red lipstick, gradually chewed off. I kept telling myself: this was not the way to meet people, it wasn't going to work; but if it was only random chance that should dictate the meeting of two people with harmonious views on birth control, the *Game of Thrones* finale and whether or not Labour had an anti-Semitism problem – all this in a city of over 150,000 – it did not seem ill-advised to see whether you could strike it lucky on another night. At Bradmore Road, my neighbour laughed at me. That was what algorithms were for. Here, he said, reaching for my phone, tapping for a few minutes; raising his arm at an angle to aim it at me. When he handed it back, I had a dating app installed. I looked back dourly at myself. Take a better picture, he opined. I said no; and what was this, anyway? How was it possible for him to use dating apps but not Twitter? He raised his eyebrows: my expectations were all wrong. Some things could not be avoided. He could ignore Twitter, but if his chance of sex was now dependent on a phone, if it was true that no one thought any more to look for other people at a bar when the whole world up to a user-established radius was ready for a swipe and a fuck in the convenient grasp of their palm, then of course he would accept dating apps. Besides, who would waste time quizzing successive candidates over drinks when a concrete profile could establish a more select coterie of people by presenting the immediate facts off the bat: height, food preference, life-changing experiences? On what more evidence did I need to drink alone? He said this; I knew all this, and yet, there was always the hope – tomorrow, at the Rose and Crown, eyebrows plucked, legs shaved, nylon sheers newly bought and a gin and tonic twirling in one, nervous hand – there will be someone.

The app my neighbour had installed depended on women making the first pass. This was meant to be a rectification of heteronormative dating practice: no need for men to play hard. It put the initiative in women's arms and freed them from passivity – or so the marketing told, but all it really did was reveal that one sex was just as stunted and awkward as the other at saying hello.

In my dreams, I was spontaneously approached, and the conversation passed easily like in tennis or chess, with pre-established rules.

Emojis, my neighbour counselled. I told him to shut up.

The app asked whether or not you were looking for a serious relationship. I thought this was a trick question of sorts and let the request go unanswered on the settings page. It also had less scope than I imagined most of its users would have hoped for – an hour was all it took to happen across the profiles of several students, fellow colleagues, my neighbour. I looked at the photos of themselves they'd deemed attractive enough to show and read their profile summaries attached below (*Male, 24, Looking to leave the single market before the UK does*). The embarrassment was dull – as though I'd intruded on something I was not meant to see, but each profile was so posed and distanced through the medium of the screen that it almost felt as if I hadn't.

At the start, I tried not to base my preferences on looks alone, but profiles weren't much to go on either. Sometimes the only redeeming feature was looks. In constructing a profile, the app required the user to answer a series of questions, which would then be visible to all. Tell me a joke, was one. In a display of feminist virtue all the men replied, the patriarchy, and then expected sex in return. But the earnest, well-intentioned ones were equally off-putting. My conversations on here aren't usually this good, said one early match. I had asked him where he was from.

What do you want? another asked. In the spirit of honesty, I told her: I was no longer sure what I was allowed to want. Everything I had been raised to desire had, at some point, become passé, but no one had told me. There was a chasm between my expectations and the reality I had to exist in which no one else seemed to grasp. When I FaceTimed home and told my parents I found it unlikely that I should ever walk into a room and meet the person with whom I would one day take out a mortgage, have a child, get a dog, make a home, they stared at me blankly. When I told my neighbour I found it unlikely that a swipe could ever incur something good, he laughed. And though I wanted to be a good feminist, be grateful for the advancements of a post-post-feminist age and #MeToo, I did not want to end up alone.

There was a long pause. The speech bubble swelled, tremored and receded, then loosed: You're overthinking it. Happiness is something you create. And homes are just things people make pretty until they can no longer afford them, or afford something better.

I stared at her response for a long time. Perhaps ours is a lost generation of sorts? I eventually wrote.

Lol, get over yourself, showed her next message, at which point I deleted the app. It's just as well, my neighbour reasoned glumly after I recounted this over a customary round of drinks. I wanted to talk about the gamification of dating, but he swayed lightly on his stool and shook his head. No wonder I couldn't get laid. But then, softening: you got a false impression of what the situation was on dating apps. Matches seldom were what they appeared on one's phone. The likely event was that we'd all end up alone.

He brightened momentarily. But he and his sort-of-girlfriend had just agreed to take a break, and since we were both out of luck, already at a pub and headed home together anyway –

Any discomfort there might have been after I rejected his offer was bypassed by the fact that, up the road, Cornmarket Street had been upturned. In the centre of it all, a girl with close-cropped hair on a white van spoke through a megaphone, but her words got lost in the wider chant of the crowd. I nudged my neighbour, who stopped to look on. His eyesight was better than mine. He looked into the scrum while I checked my phone, and like this, we put together a quick sketch of what was going on. Oxford Union. The guest for that night was a former journalist turned politician who had once been president of it himself. Over the course of his first career he had engendered various forms of hate speech, most notably against women who chose to wear a hijab. After his tenure as Mayor of London, which had cemented his platinum-blond hair and oafish smile as a cultural meme through a series of well-performed stunts – wobbling around the city on a bike two times too small for his backside; hanging off a zip wire – he had sent a bus round the country sowing improbable economics and Euroscepticism in the name of the National Health Service. I had never seen the bus in person – nor had my neighbour when I asked – but it was a widely accepted part of the news cycle online. It was enough to catapult him to Secretary of State for Foreign Affairs. Outrage politics were the thing on which he thrived.

We turned north. I checked my phone to see whether the protest had hit Twitter but a search on Cornmarket returned only a handful of eyewitness reports. I searched the Union instead. My neighbour glanced at my phone.

I read an article— oh, pardon, he said, and broke off. A beer belch rumbled out of him. He tipped his head in apology and resumed. I read an article by a bloke who went to school with him, before anyone knew he'd be mayor or Brexit minister. It was written in a rather elite newspaper. The article claimed that true ambition had silent claws; that entitlement was only fruitful when softened with charm. That was what the school they had gone to had taught. The article described aspects of the boys who had gone on to become Cabinet ministers – the character of their walk, how active they were on the playground – in a way that overstated the significance of these things in relation to the men they had become. It was the institution, not any sort of inner nature, which bred them. Dinner halls taught them how to assume the posture of being served; grounds funded by generations of their families taught them how to walk on any land as though it belonged to them. Really, my neighbour had found the angle from which the article had been written interesting in itself: the author had seen himself as sufficiently apart from the goings-on of the school to comment on them with faint bemusement or distaste. He had qualified this by the fact that he had gone to the school on a scholarship fund. His parents were working class. He did not read *The Times* or the *Sun*, preferring

61

the *Guardian* instead. But my neighbour sometimes sat in on PPE seminars which bred the kind of boys mentioned in this article, and frankly, could not discern much of a difference in tone between this article and what he heard in class. Or perhaps not so much tone, as a way of speaking. Passive liberalism was the same as Toryism. And wasn't it the case, my neighbour pointed out, that this writer had nonetheless been raised enough within the milieu of these boys that he could now comfortably live in one of the most expensive cities on earth, writing remembrances of things past? It grated on him. Didn't I find that sort of thing aggravating, too? he asked.

I kept my eyes on my phone screen and grunted. The protest on Cornmarket had finally begun to stream through. Online, the mess of bodies I'd witnessed acquired logic; voices I hadn't been able to decipher became witty poster boards accruing likes. *Pulling out doesn't stop people from coming*, and *IKEA has better cabinets*.

If you're that interested in it, go back and join, said my neighbour irritably, upset at having been ignored.

Towards the end of May, I was required to hold a feedback group for taught graduate students who wanted to express their opinion on the texts they'd been set over the past year. There was also an option to submit opinion electronically (On a scale of one to ten, how satisfied are you with your course? Do you feel the teaching you have received has enhanced the quality of your course? Please elaborate in the box below). Perhaps because of this, only five bored faces with reusable coffee cups adjacent looked towards me from tables pushed into an angular horseshoe. With a little effort, I recognised the girl with SAD, the environmentalist, the non-binary student who, alone, seemed poised with a notebook and pen to take notes. And, to the left of the room's windows – Ghislane.

We should start, I said.

Everything I saw was a confirmation. So, she was wearing a bright orange handkerchief dress and gold rings I had seen on her Instagram page. Just as I'd seen on my feed, she'd dyed her long, dark hair dirty blonde and was wearing less make-up than the night we met. She seemed unaccompanied in the horseshoe: stretching her legs out in a straight sloping line under the table and leaning her body at a right angle into her seat. Both of her hands were placed in the pockets of her jacket, which remained on. She was as still in her chair as she was on my phone. The only surprise was to find her in the soft, changing light of the spring; to see what difference it made when the sun went behind the clouds and new shadows appeared on her face in real time, then dissolved as clouds parted. I smiled in recognition. She gave a vacant nod back. I couldn't be disappointed. Only one of us had been periodically checking the other's socials for almost a year.

Ideals wrought by the twentieth century were dead, one of the graduates in a Hawaiian shirt was saying to the room. And he hadn't really seen that reflected in the course reading. In fact, they had been taught as though language hadn't developed past modernism. Frankly, he said, gathering speed, the whole premise of the catalogue they had received was lazy. They had been given *Heart of Darkness* so that they couldn't say the course hadn't covered questions of imperialism and race. They had been given *Mrs Dalloway* so that they couldn't say the course hadn't addressed feminism. But he did not want a pre-established discussion on the difference between the savage and the civilised, or on angels in the house. The question of a functioning social identity in the twenty-first century was slipperier than that. It was time to start questioning the inherent virtue assumed by minority politics. No disrespect – he raised his palms in apology, he knew his place as a cis white male in the new order – but just because a character was a woman, or brown, did not make them infallible to the basic human cruelty. Social politics now functioned at the level of the 'I'. At the very least, if the texts could not be changed, he wanted to know how the logic behind them had led to the strains of metamodernism and auto-fiction being produced now. Could I communicate that back, please? He appraised me conspiratorially, but I had been told to remain neutral; to create a safe space for student opinions so that they could be relayed authentically.

I looked at Ghislane. Her face was unresponsive. I *was* disappointed.

I agree and I don't, said the student next to him after an uncertain pause in which I failed to respond. The past was prologue. There was as much wisdom about our current situation to be found in texts written a century ago as anything being produced today.

Such as? he shot back.

The best lack all conviction, while the worst are full of passionate intensity, they cited.

64

He slumped back into his chair. Everyone always quotes fucking Yeats, he murmured.

When they milled out, the girl with SAD hung back. How are things? I asked her. She gave a pained sigh. There was more end-of-term work to be done. She was waiting for the weather to go on the up. Seasons came so much later than she anticipated, these days. The kale juice had been a good shout. Now she was going through a mango phase, a vitamin C kick. She bought it cubed, daily, ate it first thing. The routine of waking up in the morning and having an immediate destination in Magdalen Street for a box of it helped. She had tried using the time to be a good citizen and stay informed, but it robbed any pleasure she might have gained from the process. The last time she had tried, she read that May had announced her intention to resign, and the rest of her mango slid like cement down her throat at the thought of what was to come. Lately, she had found a way to compromise by listening to a podcast on current cultural affairs presented by two slightly punch-drunk blondes whose upturned sentences made any calamity into a question. With that, she could digest better. When the mango and the podcast were finished, she felt she had achieved some small thing, and could get on with the rest of her day.

Aha, I said, bored yet wanting to appear simpatico. She did not look convinced; cast the horseshoe a pitying glance.

For the record, she said, she had not agreed with anyone in the feedback group. There was no literature to rival the disintegration of language social media and digital technology had provoked. For example, last weekend, after a long absence, she had visited her parents. In the month she had been away, they had installed an Amazon Echo Dot in the house, a gadget she had always been resistant to. The turning on and off of lights now relied upon the word 'Alexa' – but something in the voice recognition of the technology had gone wrong and sometimes the AI system would perform another task entirely, make strange noises of its own accord, or simply not respond. Sometimes its coding would not account for the long, compound sentences in which her father spoke, and he would frustrate himself for hours trying to make it understand instead of simply accomplishing the task he was asking it to do himself: going out to check the weather, say, or looking up a foreign word. She hated that the thing had a human name and passably human voice, which made it seem as though it were a sentient being with the capacity to empathise with need and respond, rather than a thing which recognised command in a sequence of variously pitched sounds. It did all sorts of funny, relatably human stuff, like sing Ed Sheeran out of tune when you asked it to. On that account, she could not convince her parents to exchange the thing – in their minds, its technical error was tantamount to human error: they did not seem to realise it worked unto an algorithm that could not fix itself, rather than a sense of goodwill which would eventually compromise with them. And so when her father, having failed to get his meaning across cried, No, Alexa! I meant *this* – over and over – she felt her heart break. It was like watching Lear on the heath. More than this, she hated the thing simply for claiming the attention of the room. Her parents had taken to asking it to play lo-fi sounds, and it would blare ugly, discordant, so loud she had to shout to be heard. It made the house feel less like a home, which it didn't anyway because they lived in a fashionable district of London lined with pastel doors. Whenever she opened her own, it was probable someone who did not live anywhere near them would be on the front step, wearing something oversized that cost £19.99. They would drag stage lights and a friend with an equally oversized trashy Nikon camera along and splay themselves over the steps she carried groceries up, or stormed down after a fight with her mum.

Her lip twitched. One time, she had asked one of these girls to please stop influencing outside her home. And the girl had retorted that since this was London and she lived in such a privileged neighbourhood, she really couldn't complain. The influencer herself lived in a cramped house share with one bathroom and four other people that cost her half her pay cheque a month. If she had owned a house like this, she would have gladly shared her good luck with other people trying to make it in the world. Moreover, the influencer said, if she lived in a house that could be located behind Hugh Grant in a popular nineties film, she would be aware that her front door was a public zone. And then she had tucked away the label on her faux Louis Vuitton and gone back to her photoshoot.

It was a shit-show, the girl with SAD finished. She had left it. There was no way to win the privilege Olympics. And she could not blame someone like the influencer, however ridiculous they had been, for living so much of their life online. There was all the space you wanted there, you paid no money for it, and you could do with it whatever you chose. She remembered the earliest stages of Twitter, when she was fourteen: how furnishing her profile with the exact html shade of lilac text, the perfect banner and assorted heart symbols had been as crucial to her as decorating her room.

I did not feel like cooking. At college, I loaded up my dinner card and on my way to hall found my neighbour in the common, picking out the chords to 'Ghislane' on his guitar.

Please stop, I begged as I passed. He frowned. You've developed a really bad habit of snapping your fingers at me when you talk, he said, but leaned into the instrument, began to strum lightly, and instead: *I loved you since I knew ya – I wouldn't talk down to ya: I have to tell you just how I feel ...*

Even at the very front of the hall, it was impossible not to hear him. He had a strong, clear voice. It magnified over discs of porcelain and on the prongs of forks. It commanded everyone to pause over their food at intervals to listen. I lurched out of my chair and down St Giles.

The weather had broken at last. White dresses toured Magdalen Street. Various trees' spring refuse matted each pavement's edge. I stopped and took in the sight of a girl in an orange dress. She had draped her jacket over the high black fence of a derelict graveyard, leaning against it with a bag of pistachios under her arm. She was peeling a satsuma. Because of how she was holding the nuts, there was some awkwardness to the process. I walked towards her.

To see Ghislane from across the road was not the same as being on the same side of it, next to her. When I was beside her, it turned out that my view had been better than hers. I stood and tried to find something to admire in the Tesco that now faced us both.

They're on offer if you go in, she said, dropping peel everywhere so that she could shake the pistachios at me with one hand and insert half the satsuma into her mouth with the other. She swallowed it whole, popped the other half in and spoke through a thick layer of fruit. Shell some for me? I don't have any nails. You can help me eat them, too.

I broke open a few of the nuts and passed her the small handful. You didn't say much in the feedback session, I told her.

No, she agreed as she chewed. The sun was in her eyes. The light turned her face quizzical, wrinkled her features into a squint.

So?

She made a face at the kernels when I offered them again and shook her head. These aren't doing it for me. She frowned and motioned that I should follow her.

The air inside Tesco was clinically cool. Unassuming beige floor shone under fluorescent light. A few steps down to the right, a row of baked goods lined the wall. Without looking, Ghislane plucked a folded paper bag of standard value double chocolate cookies, wriggling her fingers for a basket. I held one out. We went on like this.

So? I pressed again. And she: I found it irritating. I think they all got most of their opinions from Twitter. Do you think it's possible to generate opinion at the rate the internet requires? I don't. We passed through fruit and veg. Rows of plums and peaches glazed in their packaging offered themselves in fours at half price. She threw a box of apricots towards me, an aubergine, some parsley.

No, I conceded. But the point was to elaborate your position on the past year, irrespective of anyone else's take. Ghislane looked at me with unconcealed disgust. Then, Your man in the Hawaiian shirt was showing off. So was everyone else. Who quotes *Yeats* in an argument? Reaction culture makes everything a moral and philosophical position. You asked them for their opinion of our reading list and they arrived with pre-prepared statements on the nature of the twenty-first century. And catching my expression, she passed me some tomatoes on the vine; amended: Exceptional circumstances, maybe. Maybe all you can expect to encounter in a room full of English graduate students is high-grade bullshit. But sometimes I want not to speak. I don't use Twitter any more, she said, because it became impossible to know what I thought on it. I read one thing I agreed with, and ten seconds later, a wholly convincing argument contravened what I'd only just established. Imagine being told you're wrong *all the time*. Imagine it being fashionable to prove people wrong. I can't thrive in that much negative energy.

I sympathised. I told her I was only half on Twitter, too: I watched everything, but only ever retweeted posts and never wrote my own. She took the basket from me and studied it. I want an egg mayonnaise sandwich, she said finally, and dumped the lot. I sent what I hoped was a pacifying shrug at the aggrieved customer assistant who had watched her do so.

Do you find it comfortable? Ghislane asked, now surrounded by industrial fridges and occupied with picking out a meal deal. Can you really say you have cogent thoughts about everything, all the time?

Between her fingers I could count a Twix, some Lucozade, water and the sandwich, before she turned the corner and dumped her second haul into a nearby freezer, fishing out ice cream instead. Pistachio. I became ever more acutely aware of the pained expressions on the faces of the store staff, but I could not bring myself to point them out to her. Ghislane brought the ice cream to her chin, tilting her face upwards in expectation of reply. I said, Of course not, and she nodded, satisfied. Here, she said, scooping the Lucozade and water out of the freezer once more and tossing them to me. The guy outside with his dog might want them. She marched us to self-checkout.

By now, I was beginning to feel lost. Have you enjoyed being here? I asked while she paid. Have you enjoyed your degree?

Of course, she said neutrally. Or, I will in a few months, when I feel nostalgic over it.

Ghislane stole cutlery from Pret, then took us down Ship Street. She ate the ice cream on the grass outside the Radcliffe Camera, and I watched. I wanted to feel there was a genuine warmth being established between us.

Do you remember meeting at the department party? I asked.

Kind of, she said.

71

Remember the day you met me outside 2 Bradmore Road?

No, she said simply, licking her spoon.

Walter Pater's house, I prompted.

Kind of, she said.

Oh. I deflated. You were taking pictures of it.

Ghislane nodded. I take pictures of everything.

Have *you* enjoyed your time here? she asked when she had finished eating and sprawled herself on the grass. Select your answer on a scale of one to ten below, where one is not at all, and ten is very much, she added, smirking with her eyes closed. I prickled; picked at the rest of her ice cream, set spoonfuls of it clinging to a blade in front of me and watched it moodily, as it dripped towards the earth.

I'll tell you something, she said at last, shielding her eyes from the sun, paying me the final bit of attention she had to muster. You look like them, even if you think you don't. And seeing the confused expression on my face, she said impatiently, You look right at home.

I thought about Ghislane's remark when my contract was up.

Packing took time. I had kept the cardboard boxes under my bed. I reflected. The longing. Always present during my stay at Bradmore Road, the wish to drop into a place, like a penny. I had wanted to be able to recognise the smell of the room as mine, and so had stretched freshly laundered bedding over the radiator and draped it over the backs of chairs; kept Darjeeling out. I left books open everywhere: the soft, aged musk of second-hand paperbacks and the sharp tang of new hardbacks. I burrowed down for long periods and forgot to open the window until the room smelt of my body, slow, unmoving – and when I had had enough, opened it so that the trees outside could waft the season in on branches: brittle air, pollen, sap, wind. These now seemed obscenely romantic ways in which to belong to a place where the downward slide of the pane and any absence longer than two days returned it to its original odour: fetid carpet, repainted walls. Not that it mattered, I was wiping it all down with disinfectant anyway to get my deposit back.

When things were mostly packed, Maria brought the Hoover up the stairs. I stacked cardboard boxes up above the floor, anywhere they would go. The bed, the desk, the chairs, the shelves. There were too many of them. In the end, I could only pick up and move one at a time around patches of carpet so that she could get to what was below. A notification had gone off on my phone and a livestream from the BBC came in and out of the room between the bursts of sound from the suck and gush of the Hoover. It was like anticlimax musical chairs; it went like this: *Life depends on compromise* – I lifted, I moved, she hoovered, pointed at the next box – *We have completed the work that David Cameron and George Osborne started* – I lifted, I moved, she hoovered, pointed at the next box – *housing ladder so that young people can enjoy the opportunities their parents did* – I lifted, I moved, she hoovered, pointed at the next box – *Grenfell Tower, to search for* – I lifted, I moved, she hoovered – *country I love*.

When it was done, Maria looked around pityingly. Need help?

Please, I said.

She produced one of her colourful rags. We cleaned the room together.

You have lots of things, she noted. I said, I'm giving most of them away. It accumulated, I don't know where from. She looked at me in a way that made me feel stupid; shook her head, took the nectarines from the windowsill and held them out, asking what she should do.

Help yourself, I said. She slipped one into the front pocket of her apron with a nod and set the other between her teeth. Then she opened the window to clean the glass. She lifted herself. Her foot sought out the desk in a practised move and found its hook, deft in its white trainer. She remained steady as she leaned out. She seemed utterly stable. Every so often, she reached for the window's casing, gripping it through the cloth and biting down as she brought the fruit away from her mouth with the other hand to chew. It was quick work. She spat the pit out into the garden below and addressed herself to me. Ready to go?

Almost, I said. What will you do? What's the plan after cleaning? She did not shift her gaze from the glass she was polishing. I'll still be here, she said. Mortification rooted me to the spot. I said nothing. She continued softly, with good humour. English houses are very messy. They always need cleaning. English people are very lazy. When I'm treated badly by someone with a messy house, I can't feel it seriously. Why should I listen to people who can't take care of where they live, and ask me instead to fix their mess?

She sprang lightly from the ledge and came back into the room. I'm the manager of the company your school uses to clean, she said. I see a lot of people your age.

They don't think they'll be cleaning for very long. I tell them, I was the same. But some English people will pay very well for a good, clean house. It is their reputation. Your school should think like this. It wouldn't be so grand if no one picked up the coffee cups and cans of drink you and your friends leave out. I take care of it, my staff does that work. But your school does not want to take care of us if we are sick and need to stay in bed. They do not pay us pensions after we have done work that means you can think all day, and newspapers can take pictures and say how beautiful everything looks.

I watched Maria begin to put her things together. The sun set low on the room, now dotted with uniform boxes. The sudden absence of my things made it sparse and gleaming. The houses on this road, she said after a pause, I do. I'm a manager, but I don't mind cleaning. Sometimes my staff tell me: our work is a lot of shame. I tell them they're wrong. They will not be noticed by ignorant people, but the room is a very important work they are doing.

Of course, I said. She smiled, thinly. You ignored me, she said. But it's not personal. I know how much of your payments on this room end up with me.

I stood, at a loss. I felt there was nothing I could say, except, Thank you, Maria.

She nodded, having taken a cigarette out of her apron and put it in her mouth. The Hoover dangled off her arm. Have those, she said, gesturing at a couple of rags and a spray bottle of disinfectant. Before you leave you can wipe everything down. And here, wait – she left the room briefly and returned with a cardboard folder full of paper. I must have looked confused because she said,

Don't forget those. Deposit form, insurance claim, inventory from beginning, inventory to do now. There are two copies – take one, leave one. Okay? Good luck.

PART TWO

II.III

Pay attention to this next page, the former copy editor said, because it's by the Editor's best friend. When you see this name, you'll know it needs to be perfect.

We were in an office. London, height of summer. Up on the third floor of a six-storey building, the wall-sized windows were thrown open, and the heat and the noise and the dirt of the city rose to meet the white-furnished room. The whole thing was open-plan, loped out in the shape of a serif capital 'I' – at one end a soundproofed glass box for the Editor, at the other, a cluster of twenty desks for marketing, and in between, four white wooden islands with twelve 27-inch high-resolution Retina display screens, back to back in rows of three. There was an employee for each one. I had blagged my way into the country's last society magazine, which, I had been informed at interview, was undergoing an unexpected renaissance with a new Editor at its helm. This, from Oxford, I had not known, but in the windows of newsagents there were, indeed, blown-up posters of the magazine's cover, each issue selling at least as well as other glossies.

You need to be careful with her pages. He will personally check everything by her, my predecessor continued. Always make sure they go straight to the top of the pile. She retrieved an A3 sheet from the printer beside her and slid it towards me; I took a Post-it, wrote, Lady P. Always Urgent. I stuck it on the side of my own giant screen, obscuring the calendar's date shining out from it: 8 July. Someone a few desks over from mine was having sushi in front of their screen. I wanted the spicy salmon roll they were eating; I wanted to be able to google Lady P.'s name and find out how she fitted in to the complicated web of marriages, rivalries and tax havens I had been studying all morning; I wanted to put her name through Twitter and find as much gossip about her as possible. Constantly, I found my mind turning on what was happening outside of the office instead of in it. I looked at the page. Lady P. had sent in a list of items and a 300-word brief on creating modern opulence in the process of interior design. I took in the £20,000 iron chandelier, £3,000 lamp, price-on-request Nureyev trolley. In the top-right corner was a photo of Lady P. in question: draped in Alice Temperley, her arms thrown out. The art director, a woman with coin eyes wrinkled at the edges and a Jane Birkin haircut neither blonde nor grey, craned her neck to look at the page. She had a soft, anxious voice.

This is a good moment to point out, she said, before you start work on it, all the things that make the architecture of the page work. You see? Those sofas are facing each other on either side, diagonally, which offsets the head and sell for the article, makes it appealing. And then you have furniture arranged on the page in a way which encourages the reader to visualise buying it all –

the lamp on top of the fireplace, and the mirror above the chair, and the wallpaper behind the sofa, and so on. It's important that they can visualise putting these things in their home. The architecture of the page – she looked up to make sure I was listening – is as much about the commercial as it is about the aesthetic. What you're looking at isn't just leisure or taste, it's product. We make a lot of revenue off these pages.

My predecessor smiled. That's right, she said. And the page furniture – the prices and headlines you'll be writing in – play a big part in that, too. She pulled out another page, this time covered in a collage of well-groomed people holding drinks, posing. She began to explain: The party pages are what we're known for; names are everything here. Names are money, and a lot of readers will buy each issue to see who's inside …

I let her go on. If you looked outside the windows and dropped your eyes, you would see the square. Periodically, outside the huge revolving doors to the building, a young woman in heels carrying an impractically sized bag would stand with her back to them and her front to a photographer, and then leave. This kind of woman who never went in was punctuated by women who did – women in long, floral dresses always paired with Birkenstocks, an iced coffee, a green juice. The square itself contained three distinct zones: a patch of green in which office workers took their lunch under its canopy of trees; a throughfare for buses and taxis; an advancing length of torn-up pavement around which men in neon jackets drilled. From the blemishless white office on the height of the third floor, the square functioned like its own, complete ecosystem.

The Editor will always want a witty, snappy, glamorous head for every page, my predecessor was saying. Those are your key words and you have to operate in that kind of universe. So, for example, this page on the Serpentine Party, he approved *Top of the Lake*.

I felt my brow contract. But that's a crime show, I said. She nodded. There was something flat about her face in spite of its dark features. Really witty, repurposing it for a glamorous social party, right, she said, and I wondered whether she was joking, or if the association between the murdered women on the show and pouting, stiff-boned women on the page really was lost on her. She looked at her phone. She was dressed more sensibly than anyone in the office.

We've got just enough time, she said, to grab a quick coffee, and I'll finish telling you what everyone does in here. Then you can go to lunch.

I had left Oxford by bus in the last week of May. Hours on it blurred. London appeared along the A40 in leisurely orbit – first fields and asphalt, then shopping centre, then that tower block, a Hilton hotel. It was non-time spent in transit. To sit and be carried somewhere with no effort, at a specified rate. To be safe in the knowledge of a destination. In the bus, I had felt cocooned: I fell asleep and woke up with my breath on the windowpane. I had checked Twitter and watched a politician's gaffe as he pretended to hold his phone in a video someone else had made for him: online, viewers said it was endearing. Things happened, but I could suspend them if I liked. When the view got boring, I drew the curtains on it.

When the snoring of my fellow passengers reached my ears, I had headphones ready to counter it.

Eventually the bus had stopped just past Shepherd's Bush and I'd walked to Barons Court where a friend of a friend had agreed to sublet her sofa for £80 a month. Past the Georgian stucco and white brickwork of West Kensington, trundling a suitcase over uneven slabs of stone in one hand and a small bouquet of crocuses my neighbour had sent me off with in the other. They must have been the last of the spring. He had presented them with a sheepish flourish and said, I will miss you, even though you are ridiculous. Sometimes it was like you were acting out how you thought we'd all like you to be.

I said, What do you mean? and his expression grew more sheepish. He said, Shit, that was terrible, I didn't mean to offend you – but I waved my hand impatiently, and he went on – You never went out. You never talked to anyone. You seemed to live on fairy meals, like boiled eggs and tangerines and honey. I could have read you in a novel. When I had to carry you out of that party I took you to last year, my friends asked where I had got to the next day. I told them about you and no one remembered your being there. They wanted me to bring you to another party, but you seemed happy enough in your room. I had to narrate you to them – sometimes they asked how you were.

I had cupped the crocuses in my palm and watched him muster himself. He said, I expect you'll be glad to be gone – off to do literature in the real world and whatnot, and on my part, I felt all the righteousness drain out of me. I suppose, my neighbour had said at the door, we probably won't speak all that much after this. People always say, let's keep in touch, but it's never the case, is it? Might be best to see how it goes. I agreed with him out loud, but in the days before I left I had already been envisioning what it would be like to visit after some period of absence: more beautiful and alive than I had ever been while actually living there, radiant with success.

Towards Barons Court, my suitcase had kept getting stuck on bits of raised pavement, stopping and starting the walk over. I hated it. I had been lied to by every woman who had ever written in a book or glossy magazine about packing a suitcase. There was no leotard and Basis soap, chicly minimised capsule wardrobe and wild-card party dress with a Celine fragrance to match. I could not pack to an itinerary; the contents of my suitcase had no coherent brand. I knew this did not make me a non-person, and still I resented the assortment of stray mints, chargers, loosely filed papers. My suitcase was a water bottle, a P60, my clothes without a wardrobe and brutal-ised with creases – but, I thought, I should not be complaining, there was always someone who had it worse than me. Whenever I forgot, I looked at my phone or self-flagellated with the *Guardian*. There was a prolifer-ation of opinions on Twitter about what it took to be a good, inclusive, progressive person, but I read such lists and threads on the cusp of going to Waitrose or preparing for sleep, whereupon they were quickly replaced with other lists: sliced bread to be bought, teeth to be brushed. When I remembered I had forgotten them, I felt like a terrible person anew. I wanted to discuss this with someone, but there was never any time. Quickly, I realised the absurd wealth of the places I had been in over the past year: rooms in which such discussions could be played with in theory, without urgency, at any time, and then set aside to be taken up at a later date. The internet was one such room: a constant, useless distress in my pocket. I had resolved to stop looking at my phone if I could help it; to turn off my notifications and live less theoretically.

The girl whose sofa I was to be sleeping on lived in what must have once been an art deco hotel: a long, dilapidated semicircle of a building with five storeys, elaborate stonework mossed over and construction railings going up against each balcony and its flat. Cosseting the building was a rusted fire escape out on which various tenants now stuck their dustbins. The driveway arched round a patch of green and some drooping palm trees. The whole thing was gated, intercommed, needed a key fob for access, but when I went to buzz at my arrival, the set of main gates swung open to let a car out, and I slipped past it.

The lifts on the ground floor still had grates; there were porters' desks, but they were empty. The stairs leading to each floor were yellowed, linoleum lined things, with the lights bouncing off them in pearlescent spots. I was on the first floor. When the door swung open, a girl younger than I had expected stood in its frame and waited impatiently. I held out four twenty-pound notes and said, I'm here about the sofa?

She looked confused; asked, How did you get in? I told her how I had arrived at the moment a car was leaving, how I had gone through the gates before they closed.

Don't do that again, she said. You can cut yourself keys and clone a fob later today. She let me into a short, narrow corridor quite agitated, saying, Don't sneak in the gates again.

The corridor opened up to a living room. Immediately I could see there was no way to get in or out of the flat without passing through it, and by extension, the sofa. There was a narrow table which seated four in theory and more probably three in practice: its wood was the same colour as the linoleum stairs. There was a dirtied grey carpet my new flatmate walked over shoeless regardless; a small cluster of cabinets with mail on top of them addressed to several different names, none of which, from the quick glance I was able to give, belonged to her. The sofa, she said, like the rest of the furniture in the flat, had been left by the landlord. It opened up into a bed, although she didn't advise it. It had been there when the previous tenant had lived here, too. She herself was not like the flat. She wore a black, carefully untailored piece of linen and statement earrings; she guided me through a kitchen with grease-stained walls and jewellery tools on the counter; a bathroom with decomposing tiles. That was the price of semi-reasonable rent, she said. In this area, there were a handful of magnificent, crumbling buildings with landlords who would lease them to you for cheap and then invoice you for damage you didn't notice when you moved in. But if you walked twenty minutes up the road, you would see maisonettes with interiors and owners beautiful enough to be featured in *House & Garden*, as though opposite each of them, on every road, there was not a council estate. *That* was worse, my new flatmate said, then caught herself and narrowed her eyes at me. Are you a Tory? I shook my head. Good, she intoned. As she had been saying, she would never want to live at such extremes. These days, everyone with a salary who wasn't an oligarch left London for the suburbs in the end anyway – and even the oligarchs left their flats unoccupied. She suspected she would leave too, but for now, she worked in a bookshop and sold rings online, so this would do.

I stood clutching my suitcase while she spoke. You're a bit sad, aren't you? she said, an eyebrow raised. I offered her a weak smile and she deepened in her disgust. It's not a personality trait, you know, she said. You want my advice, stop moping and go *make* something. *Do* something. She threw a set of keys at me with a deft hand.

My rings, she said, get carried around. They live beyond me, tangibly. It's transcendent, you understand? They're not just material things: they're a way I become something meaningful in other people's lives. It's something beyond my everyday self. And it's a nice wad of extra cash each month. Anyway, she nodded at the keys, you'll need sheets. I haven't got any to spare. You'll need to cut yourself keys. Those ones are mine and I'll need them back today. And you'll need to do your own shopping. Will you find your way around?

I said yes, I had lived in London before.

Good. Off you go, she said, and disappeared into her bedroom.

On Kingsway, the linden trees were the only thing that calmed me. I knew them well. My flatmate had suggested a locksmith in Chelsea, but I thought it was possible she was right: that what she took to be sadness was, in fact, my anxiety at being back in the city with no discernible plan. Holborn was a familiar place where life had once had reliable form: I wanted sanctuary. I cut a copy of the keys. I cloned the fob. Then, at the very end of the road, I walked across towards Bloomsbury, found Tottenham Court Road, bought sheets, bought tinned cannellini beans, tangerines, almonds, coffee, and, in spite of myself, a second-hand book. I took it all to Russell Square and unsheathed it beneath the cool, intimate shade thrown onto the grass by the yew, the oak, the Scots elm. The idea had been to read for a while.

I checked Instagram. I checked on Ghislane, but she was no longer posting. She remained, still, in gridded squares, in common rooms, in libraries, in three-minute clips of a popular nineties song. I lay on the grass and listened to her namesake.

I texted my mother. She wrote, I suppose there's no point asking you to take a train home, and my stomach did its little guilt squeeze, answered, I still need to look for a job.

Years ago, I had studied around Bloomsbury. In Oxford, it had held the idealised sheen of a former home, but now, with the knowledge that I would have to pay for any amenity around it that would make me comfortable – a toilet, a drink – to sit there was unbearable. I could not find it in me to think that amenities would have to wait.

Unfortunately for you, the former copy editor said, sketching out a rough floor plan when we had settled in the cafe, your main concern is everything and everyone. Don't lose this – she slashed a rectangle into three desks and above it drew another; carried on, until there were several – and don't show it to anyone. When she was done, the office we had just come from was laid out, crude in 2D and biro over a stained napkin. The hum of espresso machines and shouted orders dimmed her voice. I strained to hear her.

So, she breathed out, and began tapping her pen over the corresponding desks as she spoke. You'll want to know that her father is in the House of Lords, *she* used to sleep with every musician you can think of in the nineties, and *her* sister does PR at Buckingham Palace. This guy here, his wife is the former editor of the magazine upstairs. What else...? He went to uni with a bunch of royals. Ah, and she's about to marry into acting royalty. The rest of them are normal, but either they've been there longer than you've been alive, or they're working pretty much for free. She pushed the napkin at me and said, It's horrible describing them all that way, but you can't be caught off guard. They're all charming, but you'll need to watch yourself. I hope you don't mind my saying so, but you look a bit clueless. I looked you up, nothing showed up about you in terms of connections or fame. I shook my head. She sighed again and asked, half-heartedly, where I was staying.

I'm on a casual contract, I explained, examining the napkin. The managing editor told me to check in with her at the end of each week to see if I'm still needed. I'm on a sofa for now.

I thought as much, she said. *Don't* lose that. If you do well here, there's a good chance they'll be too lazy to replace you and you'll become permanent staff. You'll be the only copy editor on the desk, as it is.

I nodded as though it had all made sense, which it hadn't. The job description had specified a command of English, proficiency in InDesign; none of what I'd just been told. I wanted to ask more questions but could scarcely think of what might be useful to know any more, and before I had time to think, she waved me off to lunch. So I walked west towards Hyde Park, then doubled back on myself, despondent. On the way back, a man winked at me from the ground and said, You have a good night, girls, keep smiling – but it was mid-afternoon, and there was only one of me, and I was not smiling. I blurted out, You too, and wondered whether he understood any more of the exchange than I did. When I returned to the office, I saw the former copy editor was already there, the same coffee cup she had been drinking out of in the cafe now on her desk barely touched. I slid into the desk next to hers. Outside, the construction workers had returned from their lunch and the irregular sound of drilling filtered up from below.

In academia, so much of my work had been tied up in my moral self. I weighed up the value of a particular narrative for a living and attached my name to what, in theory, I would have the world be like. This was nothing like that. To the sound of slabs being taken up from the ground below, I proofed and revised a Cotswolds heiress's guide to laying a table: she made suggestions like putting flowers in jam jars and sitting on hay bales; her silverware was artfully tarnished. There was no need for the old formalities, she said. She encouraged her guests to turn whichever way they liked and chat away across the table – or even to move away entirely from their assigned seats. I gave it a head: *The lady is for turning.*

There was an at-home interview with a celebrity facialist whose photoshoot was overlaid with yellow boxes: in capital letters the art department had written, MAKE BRIGHT, PUNCHY, OPEN on her purple velvet sofa and her taut, gleaming skin. The interview ran over. Keep the stuff about her being an immigrant, the features editor mused on consultation, and cut the stuff about her house. I was given a page full of chintz cushions and deliberately scuffed tables: country chic was back, and every house was full of it. Rid yourself of stainless steel and loud colours, the copy advised – such things were the height of pretension. I laboured over filling in the brand names and prices: a Jo Malone wood sage candle, a Le Creuset dish. There was a couture report with gowns inspired by ancient Rome; I changed a BC to AD in red pen, and then on-screen. A few times the art director stopped me with her winding neck, her breathy vowels cutting short when she said, *Don't* move anything on the page. *Don't* change the layout, it's very specifically done. If you can't make room for it, it doesn't belong there.

I envy you your job, I said to my flatmate after my first week. Mine is all a sham. No one in my office would be able to report on the life of the one per cent if they weren't either part of it or hustling on the side. The intern sells pills. The features editor gets sent clothes by upcoming brands and they pay her for pictures of her wearing them online. I looked at her glumly. You're among books. You've got the best job in the world.

You really need to wake up, my flatmate said after a pause. I don't moon around and think and read all day. They're goods with a price printed on them. I haven't read most of them, mainly because I don't have time to. They get delivered in blue plastic crates by guys on minimum wage and I break my back lifting them, getting them onto a trolley and then arranging them on a shelf so that some fucker can take them down and leave them lying around somewhere under his discarded coffee cup for me to pick up. The owner of my company tells my colleagues and me it's a noble job and we get paid in *honour* for doing it, but honour doesn't pay my bus fare. If I could get more stable commissions for the jewellery I make, I'd leave bookselling in a heartbeat. The staff turnover in my shop has a monthly rate and people leave crying; meanwhile, the owner sits in a town house in Marylebone and cuts himself a million-pound pay cheque every year. You do not want my job. She peered at me over the remains of her dinner. Are you sure you're not a Tory?

I'm not, I said. I'm just adjusting to something new.

Oh. She grimaced. No offence. I suppose that's a bit weird to assume of a BAME person anyway. I just meant from a class perspective. But maybe Oxford will do that to you, right? I don't think you should miss it. She paused. Don't you think it's weird that you spent a year giving yourself to the place that started the careers of people that openly disdain you, and now you've gone to work for a publication that exalts them?

I had only been gone a year, but the city felt different. A month passed and still I could not root myself in it. I jumped at every face, every engine, hurling itself forward. The Tube roared out of its tunnel. I became one of those people who feared being pushed under it. In

92

Oxford I had missed the anonymising height of the buildings in London. Now they bore down on me, and everywhere, a relentless modernity. The lights were never off.

In the first weeks of moving back, before I had started my job, things were defined by what they were not. The screech of foxes in the city at night was not the thrum of crickets in Bradmore Road's overgrown grass and, however hard I tried, I could not reconcile the prevalence of shop windows to the stained honeycomb of the walls I was used to in my head. Only the private gardens were recognisable in spirit. Then gradually, the appearance of the same chains – the hipsters with backpacks and the rushed businessmen in Pret; the Zara on the high street where the girls were photoshoot-ready. Familiar patterns evolved, so at first, I had tried to get some transposition involved. I made up the sofa with cotton sheets; I woke up to Greenwich pips. But, too soon, it became a drag to fold and snag the thin white layers; to snap and unfurl them, then spread, like cold butter over cheap cardboard toast, the mass onto the sofa's fraying edge, then spread and hold myself, briefly, with arms and legs splayed, before cramping up to have my limbs fit my new bed. Only to gather it again in the morning: a sofa was a semi-public thing – my flatmate would want to sit on it, too. I gave up making it up: I threw the cushions from its back to its side: a quick displacement that took two seconds to fix the morning after. I stuffed the sheets into one of the cabinets: it was summer, I did not need covering anyway, I repeated nightly to myself, I did not need covering anyway. And when my back gave up its complaints, had acclimatised, I found a new way to get on. In the first weeks of June, I spent each morning embarrassed. My flatmate was an early riser with no compunction: she saw my sleep-swollen face, the slipped T-shirt, uncovered nipple, the furred tongue and unbrushed hair – she looked at all of this having already brushed her teeth. Cheer up, she said. People used to move all the time. You're in your natural hunter-gatherer state, cheer up, it's not like you're homeless.

I learned to get up before her by leaving the curtains open to the living-room windows. I left before she woke; the kitchen was covered in tools and the dust of semi-precious metal, I got my coffee elsewhere.

I tried spending those early mornings taking the Piccadilly Line to Leicester Square and switching over for the Northern line to Goodge Street: I had nowhere to go but Bloomsbury, no way to spend my time but minding a cardboard cup slopping cheap filter over its plastic disc on top. I tried street haunting, but could not walk for the blue-plaqued success of the dead. At dentist offices, embassies, car rental agencies, university buildings and bookstores – statesmen, architects, pioneers of women's suffrage, prime ministers, authors, artists had all *lived here*, and because of this, the price of rent in the area meant I never would. Instead of feeling free to ramble, I felt dread. The Tube was too expensive. I gave up street haunting.

Occasionally I got texts from friends who had heard I was back in the city and asked me out for drinks. But I had no cash to spare; nowhere to host them, and so demurred, promising to get back in touch at a later date. I wanted to be able to invite them to a proper flat; to have four bottles of wine resting idly in their rack, and to pull them out in succession between a starter course, a main, dessert. I tried typing out, I'm broke, and found it was too much to have on-screen privately, even after I'd found the requisite emojis to turn it into more of a joke. I left those drafts unsent. Gradually, the texts stopped coming.

I missed being an academic, and so I read. My great comfort was a particular kind of novel which seemed to be gaining traction in the publishing industry and on bestseller lists. I could not afford them as new hardbacks, but I asked my flatmate to bring proofs back from work whenever she found them. In this kind of novel, the protagonist was always a woman and always sad. At some point, she always mentioned losing her appetite and drinking coffee sweetened with cream and too much sugar instead of having breakfast or lunch; then other characters, or she herself, would remark flippantly on how thin she was. This protagonist had oblique, troubled relationships with men and spent a lot of the book's plot doing only one thing, but doing it well: sleeping, driving, smoking, going on holiday or having conversations at length – all the while making general observations under very specific circumstances as a veiled way of saying something about the nature of womanhood. The protagonist was inevitably compared to the author. This last thing was what made these books popular: it was revolutionary for a woman to spend 250 pages looking at herself in some way. These books were always written in sparse, spiky prose that ebbed my spare hours away. It was their specificity I admired – their descriptions of buttons on coats, macadamia nuts next to beds. Whatever problems these women had were bound up in their material existence: the more beautiful their circumstances were, the more pleasure I took in absorbing their turmoil. A central character in one of the books equated the dishevelment of her inner life with the renovation of her house for 260 pages. Between applying for jobs, I lay on my flatmate's mouldering sofa for the month of June and read ceaselessly.

Also popular during this time were long-form essays published in book form by women who said the way to vote when the time came would be Lib Dem, advocated centrism and wore Shrimps coats: 10,000-word chapters on breaking up with your iPhone, the tyranny of yoga, the tyranny of Amazon, the conversation they had had with their non-binary-non-white friend which had changed their perspective on – not to sound dramatic – *everything*, why loneliness was a valid form of existence, why they had checked their privilege, why they could be a feminist and still enjoy the unique pleasure of a Net-A-Porter delivery, and a list of all the times their life had gone wrong – those times had made them the strong woman who had written the book you were holding today. If you liked the book, you could also buy merchandise on their website; buy tickets to live recordings of their podcast at Liberty or Selfridges. My flatmate brought these books back to roll her eyes at: she read paragraphs out loud over dinner and snorted between commas. When she did, I began to feel self-conscious about my perverse enjoyment of them, but they, along with the novels I was reading, began cropping up on my Instagram feed, their attractive covers decorated in sans-serif font posed decoratively at an angle on a wooden table next to coffee and flowers, or arranged in cotton sheets on someone's bed. Occasionally, I found a crossover between the two genres: non-fiction in which the author found kinship with a writer, usually dead, usually with a legacy of radical politics. Writers who had worked as street hustlers, who had had abusive parents, who had been vagrants, who had died of Aids, who had had MI5 dossiers made in homage to their activism, who had been barred from entire countries, whose legacies now functioned in the machinations of north London suburbia: the particularly feminine plight of taking one's children to school; the trauma of swilling Moët at the reception of your own wedding; the drudgery of one's husband managed through gardening as a form of therapy and then recycled into a paying crowd at a Bloomsbury bookshop. I read these books attuned to each page in the same way some people watched police procedurals or medical dramas. My flatmate sent me interviews with each author once I'd finished: tasteful videos or photoshoots in which such women discussed the theoretical impossibility of the home from behind the marble island in her kitchen, or described the eighties prints above her fireplace as 'the spirit of the room'. More than I cared to admit, I wanted to know what the contents of each writer's fridge was; how she arranged the papers on her desk. It was of key interest to me to notice how, by her front door, she and her family stacked their shoes, and to note what brand of perfume was in her bathroom. This was not my flatmate's concern on the matter. *Ffs*, read the accompanying commentary to each link. *Could these women be at least a little subtler while they monetise the evolving identity politics of the left and turn them into bored Lib Dem housewife interior design strategies?*

When in July I finally secured my job, I took up my spare hours differently: I went out on foot at 7 a.m. and watched carefully what went on around me. London, the workshop. London, the machine. I walked a straight line of an hour and a half alongside the A315: first Persian cafes, bodegas with wasps pushing into pomegranates and Medjool dates stacked outside, then charity shops and alleyways breaking off into mews flats until it all became the Kensington High Street – overripe with French patisseries, pizzerias, a Cos, a Uniqlo, Whole Foods. At that time of day there were delivery trucks and bin men going by in the pale light: au pairs waiting outside Waitrose for the glass doors to slide open on cue. I saw it all in passing for a minute at most a day. After Knightsbridge, the series of hotels: past the tinted windows of One Hyde Park, in quick succession, the doormen of the Mandarin Oriental, the Berkeley, the Ritz all tipped their hats at me with white-gloved hands. I carried their salutes up through Piccadilly. The only bend came through the turn into the Burlington Arcade: antique jewellery glittered in its cage and Savile Row announced itself scented with after-shave at the end. Below the suited mannequins, under each shop the sliver of a window in the gutter of the street gave way to the scurrying of tailors. Once I hit the office building, I tapped my key card against the magnetised strip by the door, and I was let in. At the end of the day, I made sure my key card was tucked into the pocket inside my bag and walked the same route back to Barons Court.

It's a £65 day rate, the managing editor said in my first week. Sorry, I should have mentioned.

I heard myself saying, No, of course, thank you for telling me; I'm just here to do a good job – and almost meant it. I could not do anything to impede my chances of a permanent contract. But later, scrolling through Rightmove, dull panic turned practical. £700 on a room, zone 2 or 3, only to find I would still not be able to afford my life. Then hours lost to dream criteria. If I clung on long enough to secure a proper salary at the magazine, then maybe: a flat to myself, where I could feel unembarrassed about how I looked in the morning, would not have to wait to use the bathroom, or regularly find the washing machine loaded with dirty laundry. But the idea could not form credibly in my mind. Already, the more realistic prospect of a long-term flatshare had turned into wishful thinking. To my flatmate, on the same salary as me, How do you afford it? And she, barely audible and throwaway, My parents. If you can, you'll end up doing it too. There's no other way to stay.

Although I took pains to come in early and work late, the Editor of the magazine was absent for another two weeks. When the former copy editor left, she put a microfibre cloth and room spray on my desk. That's more for him than it is for you, the picture editor said in response to my confusion. He likes a tidy office. You'll know when he's due because you'll get a bollocking about the state of your workspace.

It was true. When an email emerged in mid-July asking us pointedly to keep all personal possessions off our desks, orchids appeared on each window's ledge, pale and hovering. The intern was tasked with keeping them alive. They checked each fragile petal with an anxious face, whispering, How do you know if they need something? This was the general state of things. A couple of days prior, the art director had spilt a flat white on the carpet beside her desk; now production was usurped with the process of negotiating with a cleaner over the phone. I've been calling for two days now, she said into it, more agitated by the hour, I've got a stain that's really quite urgent.

On 19 July, three days after the orchids appeared, I watched him blow into the office – sunglasses on his head, swathed in the customary ill-fitting clothes of the expensively dressed. The hems of his jeans and sleeves were too short and everything else, somehow, conspicuously loose. He went into the soundproofed glass box of his office for half an hour, then blew back out. His assistant, a small woman who sent the smell of plain miso wafting downwind towards my desk punctually at one o'clock every day hovered behind him. At his presence, the room became supine. He kissed the associate editor in the European style and with the voice of a true Sloane purred, You looked *so* good at the Cartier last night. *So* good. I was only there for fifteen minutes, if you stay any longer at a party then it's probably dead, but I saw you there looking *so* good.

She, far older than him, gave him a luxuriant chuckle and the affection of a great-aunt. Where have you been? she asked. It's been just hell for me.

He made sure to widen his eyes. Oh?

Look. She gestured extravagantly towards the large, open window beside her desk. Look. Thames Water dug up the road in front of my house and now these bastards, I don't know who they're with, have dug up the road here, and all I hear from the moment I wake up to the moment I go to sleep is the sound of a fucking drill. Look, I recorded it on my phone, what they're doing by my front garden—

She was a foot shorter than him. When she leaned in to show him the video on her phone, her shoulder brushed the crook of his elbow: the phone could not have reached his line of sight. She, squinting at the screen, tapped the play and pause button in quick succession with her index finger so that the recording kept stopping when she meant it to start. That's arduous, the Editor quipped drily.

It is, it's real hell, she returned. So do you know what I've done? I've checked into the Berkeley and sent Thames Water my bill.

That's good, he said, his attention already lost. There's a piece in there, we've got so much interiors stuff in this issue anyway. It would be good to do a one-eighty on that, you know? Write me something about your life without a home. We'll call it something like 'Nowhere Land'. Actually no, we won't call it that, but think about it, would you? And there *is* something else. I want to do a bright young things feature – you know, like new debs. Do you know if any of your nineties toy boys had kids? If you can think of a list, we'll set up a time to talk. He was already on to the travel editor: and where had she got that fabulous tan from? His assistant turned to the associate editor and began running a manicured nail down a Smythson diary. I went blissfully ignored.

You mustn't take it personally. You're young, you know, the art director said once he had retreated back behind the transparent walls at the end of the room.

You're the nobody now. Christ, I remember when I was the nobody. She leaned back in her swivel chair. I was at the Slade, and to be honest with you, that degree did fuck all for me, but I remember it gave me free time to go and rage against Thatcher and the like. And then I tried to start selling some prints, but as I say, I was a nobody, so they didn't sell. I came here after that. It's actually kind of a laugh. I mean, it wasn't then – you felt it all to be very serious, and I was there, screaming about feminism and a woman's right to her own body. But I mean – I went out there in the street and now I get trolled by young women online who post pictures of my work and write about how it's of no benefit to them. That's a very narrow-minded view, she said, suddenly brisk. Just because I work on a society magazine. I don't even believe in the thing. Not that I'm speaking directly about you, but where your generation is concerned, all I see is a lot of shouting on Twitter and not much else. Anyway, what I was getting at was, you can just use this time to rage, figure out what you want your world to look like—

The phone on her desk rang. She picked it up and after a few seconds sighed into it; said, Oh don't come now. He's in the office now, the whole point was to get it cleared up so he wouldn't notice. I'll phone you when he leaves again. Then she sagged in her chair and looked over at me. Are you going to the pub?

The pub? I checked the time in the corner of my screen. There were, ostensibly, two hours left in the working day. On my desk, the mess of proof articles to fact-check, copy-edit, then send for approval, had been arranged into two neatly stacked piles. What they had gained in height, they had gained in menace: they were like little towers, could not be conquered, would not let me leave my seat.

Didn't you get what's-their-face's email?

At the desk in front of me, I watched the intern's body turn incrementally, suddenly stiff.

No. I took the next proof to be edited from the pile and tried to keep my tone light. I don't think I was cc'd in.

Oh. Well. The art director shrugged. Go anyway. Round the corner on the left, as you head to Savile Row. Big pub. You won't miss it. I won't be there, mind. But you younger lot, you always need a few drinks to cope.

Even to myself, I seemed thin-lipped. There was a jibe on my tongue about being too overworked and under-paid to afford the many litres of alcohol I needed to deal with being too overworked and underpaid, but I tapped one of the piles with my pencil and said, We'll see. My inbox lit up a few minutes later with a single line, it said, *Apologies! Forgot to cc you in. The pub is on Maddox Street. Come as you are after work.* But it was not like the chain of emails visible above, back and forth banter in lower case and textspeak among the office at large. My brain could not forgive the formality of the message sent only to me, and the relaxed warmth apparent between everyone else. I didn't reply; worked late, and went home. I was not asked to the pub again.

On 23 July, the entirety of the pavement in front of the thoroughfare and outside of the office was ripped out, save for a thin footpath leading up to the revolving doors. The rest was cordoned off. The surface area left was not wide enough to handle the two-way traffic funnelling in and out of the building, let alone the hordes of young women who still gathered insistently in front of it, simply cropping their photos to new angles. The collective temper of the office rose sharply up.

Enough with the fucking drill, the associate editor snapped at the brief burr of machinery that operated within her range of sound, and the intern, red-faced: Sorry, it's the coffee machine. I was making an espresso. Does anyone else want one? From my desk, I could see the editors in the office at large ready to reply, but when they opened their mouths a succession of grainy recordings issued into the air.

I was brought up, in my father's house, to believe in democracy. Trust the people. The sound was broadcasting from the iMac in the rightmost corner of the room. It continued – *We are masters of our fate. The task which has been set us is not above our strength; its pangs and toils are not beyond our endurance. As long as we have faith in our cause and an unconquerable willpower, salvation will not be denied us.* In front of the screen was the senior editor, a wry, jovial man with wisps of grey hair, who leaned back and watched it with the air of taking in a good football match. The office began to gather around him and the voices of Conservative ministers past to play a game, could they identify each voice? First Churchill, and now –? The managing editor reached towards the keyboard and increased the volume. *It's a proud thing, to be given the office of Prime Minister of Britain. As for courage, character – I know the British people have these in full measure. Britain has been great, is great, and will stay great, providing we close our ranks and get on with the job.*

It was impossible to get a good view. Those who had already descended on the screen obscured it completely. I stood on tiptoe, felt absurd, and listened as best I could. *I have only one thing to say*, the speakers issued next, *you turn if you want to.* And laughter. *The lady's not for turning. I will not change just to court popularity. I am happy that my successor will carry on the excellent policies that in fact have finished with the decline of socialism and have brought great prosperity to this country, which have raised Britain's standing in the world and in fact have brought about a truly capital-owning democracy.*

What is 'Maggie Thatcher'? said the intern. The senior winked at them; stretched his arms; placed his hands behind his head. As he did so, a space cleared where the editors had parted to make way for his gesture. I caught a small rectangle of a view. There was a seated audience in front of a banner of blue, and intermittently the screen cut to two empty chairs. The senior editor yawned, and the audio clips, overlaid with a gently swelling piano track, went on.

I believe that when our children and grandchildren look back on this turbulent century, they'll look on those years from 1979 onwards and say, these years changed the face of our nation; they changed the fate of our nation, and they changed them both for the better. The yawn was contagious. It spread while the piano morphed into a chorus of violins: the sort of thing played at the denouement of war movies. The intern, having finished their espresso, fiddled with their vape, and the features editor, who had only just come into the room with her lunch, ate standing – a Niçoise salad, and the crunch of lettuce leaves, the tang of tuna behind me.

Is this it? she asked, picking tomato out of her teeth. Have they announced it yet?

No, the senior editor said, swivelling round to face her and grinning broadly. They're just having a bit of foreplay over a gramophone.

It's not just foreplay, I said. They're writing him into the books. I wanted to speak more; express my anxieties about an election I had no say in, and which I had been told repeatedly by various news outlets had only one outcome. But the features editor had jabbed her fork at the screen and asked, Who's this now? Everyone looked at her instead; began discussing, genially, the cast of characters onstage. It was impossible to take in. On the senior editor's screen: pseudo-democracy and spectacle for a man who had called the people he was set to govern piccaninnies and letter boxes. Around the senior editor's screen, lunchtime banter, low laughter, gossip, calm. The world turning as it ever did, as though nothing very much was happening.

This is terrifying, I murmured. I don't see how, the senior editor said mildly, and then the screen dispensed, *Ladies and gentlemen, please welcome—*

I pulled my attention back to it. There, considerably tidier than the photos of him riding around the city on his bike, hanging on a zip wire, giving the thumbs up after his visit to the Oxford Union, was the politician with his platinum hair and oafish smile. The camera cut to the two vacant chairs again, and held there as he and his competitor took their seats. I watched the senior editor tap the rightmost side of his keyboard to drive the volume still further up.

This is it, the associate editor said, rubbing her hands together and straining, next to me, to see. The room fell quiet to give way to the sound of *declare that the total number of eligible electors was 159,320. The turnout in the election was 87.4%. The total number of ballot papers rejected was 509. And the total number of votes given to each candidate was as—*

From the square outside, the sound of drills cast itself once more abruptly into the room. The senior editor tapped insistently at the corner of his keyboard again, but the volume, already as high as it would go, remained drowned out by groan of steel against stone, changing only in pitch as the machines burrowed in at new angles to the ground below. It screeched: the screen cut to the two men, sombre, turned in the same direction, dumb and blinking as they sat. The drill deepened – the one with the platinum hair said something, rose, shook his opponent's hand. The drill roared, and everyone on-screen began to stand, beating their hands together, and in front of the new Prime Minister, several men emerged with Dictaphones, with iPhones, with cameras; he said something else, gave the thumbs up, began to move towards the stage. The senior editor, by now quite irate, motioned me to close the windows across the room. One by one, as they shut, a bouncing, conversational voice filtered in, strengthening as each latch went. I began at the back of the office. Briefly, before the burst of another drill, I heard, *question the wisdom of your decision. And there may even be some people here who still quite wonder what they have done*. I closed the first window and found I had to circumvent the islands of each desk and then stretch above them to bring the panes down. I paused to listen again, and heard, *the instincts to own your own house, your own home, to earn and spend your own*

107

money, to look after your own family. I knocked my knee on the corner of one of the desks and cut my hand with a jagged latch. I wanted, less and less, to carry on, but the senior editor nodded at me and said, it's working. I closed another, and then wrapped my palm in a tissue. I went on. *Do you feel daunted?* the voice asked. Another window closed. I felt the tissue start to unravel from my palm and stopped to re-bandage my hand. I caught, *we are going to defeat Jeremy Corbyn*, and then, nauseated, refocused my attention to get to the next window. By the middle of the room, I could more or less hear the sound issuing from the speakers of the senior editor's desk in its entirety. *Some wag has already pointed out that deliver, unite and defeat was not the perfect acronym for an election campaign, since unfortunately it spells dud – but they forgot the final 'e', my friends, for 'energise'. And I say to all my doubters, dude, we are going to energise the country.* I made it back to the huddle. The senior editor was no longer looking at the screen.

Bit weird, him saying 'dude', isn't it? the intern mused. A bit shambolic compared to all the other speeches they played in the run-up. They began to shrug their jacket on, declaring, Well, if that's done, I'm heading out. The Wolseley, if anyone wants to come. Think about it. You'll all get wrinkles if you stay here frowning like that and we know how our fearless leader feels about those. Ciao ciao.

Momentarily, I was distracted. More than anyone else in the office, I had assumed the intern was like me: skint, and trying very hard to be kept on board. How can they afford the Wolseley? I asked. I can't afford that. What pay are they on?

No one answered. The office, having barely altered in aspect or pace, processed the country's new reality in its own, leisurely way. Text from you-know-who, the features editor said. Anyone with connections to the new PM from school, or friends, or family, please email him, he wants to get a clear picture of the social web we're working with now. The digital editor turned to her deputy. Being PM won't make him more photogenic, she mused, I don't think we'll get any engagement with images of him. See if you can pull together a style file on his girlfriend, she's not bad-looking, and maybe see if you can find the write-up we did of his old school; update the metadata on it for any potential clicks we can get. The deputy was already buried in her phone. Yep. There'll be photos of him bowing at Her Maj's hand over the next few days as well – I'll stay on the lookout for those. See if we can do a short one on any shade she throws with her clothing, you know: EU brooch or anti-Tory earrings or something. The senior editor chuckled. I wonder, he said, whether that hasn't been done too many times before. We should try something else. Something audacious.

I made a conscious effort to slacken my jaw and left. At my desk, where I had left them, were the same pages I had been working on since the morning; the mess of biro pens, mechanical pencils, Post-it notes, keyboard, gum, printouts, notebooks, flatplans. None of it had changed. The art director sat stone-faced in front of her iMac, scrolling through Twitter. I rolled my chair over to her.

You didn't want to watch?

No. Why would you? None of us are the kind of people to be hit hardest by it.

It matters, I said, shocked. She grimaced, though her voice stayed even.

Sure, but how? The part of Brexit you'll feel will only benefit you. The market might crash, but you won't notice it – you've been living in austerity without knowing it for years. You're not an immigrant, you have no trouble finding a place to live. When the housing crisis hits, all you'll see is your rent go down. You're middle class – your freedom of movement doesn't end, it just becomes inconvenienced. The only thing you might really find is nutjobs having an easier time making life hard for you because you're not white, but then again, you've been at the same school they have, you work at the magazine they read. You even dress like you vote their way when you come in to work here.

I became indignant. You're not really saying, I shot back, I should just sit down and let 'nutjobs' find it easier to give me a hard time? Anyway, I'm not just thinking about myself. I traversed my brain for what I'd read, and triumphantly pulled out, What about the reformation of basic rights that will be in the hands of a government I don't trust after we leave the EU? What about rights of workers already being exploited in a zero-hour contract job, or the bodily rights of women already suffering through period poverty? The art editor cocked her head at that.

Don't shout. And stop regurgitating headlines in abstract, that's precisely what I mean. You need to start being a bit more honest with yourself when you read your daily news intake. A lot of us don't care about the decline of humanitarianism and the worsening state of the world when we watch election live streams or PMQs.

We watch it to feel good about ourselves when we tweet our dismay, or at least you lot do. All these people on here – she threw her chin towards her screen – that's what they're doing now.

That's terrible, I said flatly.

You're not listening to me, the art director said, finally losing her patience. The soft, quavering quality of her voice went short. I'm saying, stop staring at the large screen in order to pick out what you can caterwaul at on the small one in your pocket. The reason to care is not to know what happens in the abstract realm of some-body else's tweets, or to talk and talk and talk about how it affects people you've never met, and actually don't know anything about. The reason to care is to know the why of what's happening to the cost of your bread, or the electricity bill in your house. Because when you know that, you'll know how to make the system work for you. That's what matters to you.

I care about other people. And I don't think I'd presume to know what matters to you, I told her. Brexit costs me opportunities in my life.

All right, she said. Fair enough. So, when you voted for your MEP in the European Parliament elections a couple of months back, tell me, who did you vote for, and why?

I bit my lip and knew the reply. I had not voted; I had been picking through my belongings at Bradmore Road, deciding what would go into a suitcase and what would not. It would not turn out favourably for me. The art director, seeming to sense this too, relented, sighed. I know you've got good intentions at heart, she said. But you want my opinion? Either read the papers with a bit more self-interest in mind, or find some charities you can donate a few pennies to, and try not to tweet about it when you've done that. Do both, if you can.

I shook my head, downcast. Then on impulse: I've been staying on a friend's sofa lately. It's just been hard to keep up.

She softened. That's the way it is, she said. I did a few sofa hops in my time. Look, you're young. Just keep a cool head and keep at it with your work, we can all see you're trying your best here.

Okay, I said, drawing myself up and starting to organise my desk. What should I do now?

Whatever you were doing before, she said. But all afternoon, I felt guilty, I fidgeted, tried to find something else I could do, except turn the notifications back on to my phone.

II.II

That Friday, the final Friday of the month, I did not get paid. It's pretty common, the managing editor said, for there to be a lag in payroll if the employee joins after the cut-off date.

But, I said desperately, I thought I had joined before then. She gazed at me. She had an uncommonly pretty face, framed by thick, blonde hair she twirled around both hands. From behind it, the rings on her fingers waxed and waned: a gold signet engraved with her initials flashed, was obscured, then resurfaced alongside a large oval stone nestled above a gold band. You will get paid in arrears, she said at last. You don't need to worry about that.

I tried not to cry. Yes, but – I took a breath – my bank account is in double digits now.

The managing editor paused. Well, it would be a shame if you had to leave, she said, and I, with requisite terror at the message received, began calculating, as quickly as I could, the cost of a bag of rice and the portion count a tin of beans and a tin of tomatoes would stretch, the size of my flatmate's freezer and how much bread I could reasonably store. If I could beg her to pay my contribution to council tax and bills for the next month late, if I could borrow more from my parents, then perhaps...I took a deep breath. Just below my temples, I could hear a loud, insistent thrum. I counted the objects on the desk in front of me in an attempt to calm down: the Smythson diary, the wireless mouse, Chanel Huile de Jasmin, the almond butter, the two-ring binder with proofs I had assembled the previous day. I took another breath and let it out.

No, of course, I understand, I said. I really value my position here. I took a breath, and then tentatively, If there's a possibility of a small advance to help me manage until pay for next month is put through, I'd really appreciate it. I'd be very grateful. The managing editor smiled. I'll talk to HR, she said, and see what they say.

I went back to my desk; fiddled with my phone. I waited.

But I had turned the notifications back on my phone. The push alerts came, blooming kiss upon kiss, in oblong waves onto my home screen. The way apps moved had a lightness, an aerodynamics to them: they hovered, hung, bobbed in and out of view. I experienced a fog. I experienced slips in time. I looked down at my phone: on-screen it was always *now*; I looked back up, *now* was an hour later. I looked, more and more, idly fed whatever nerve filled at my swiping, at the anticipation of viewing whatever was delivered. I revived, then dulled at my thumb and its pull-down, release and refresh of mailbox, timeline, feed, waiting to see who was there, what was there to claim my attention. Algorithms were alive and well: the first notification I got was a post on Twitter, suggested because it had been liked by several users I followed. It contained a screenshot of a Facebook page called 'Memory Lane' and above it, the caption, 'Can someone please explain?!' The screenshot was a box of text; it had an Instagram filter no one used any more from years back when the platform had first started. Insistently artificial, it dirtied and framed whatever it overlaid to make it look as though the digitally generated contents were, in fact, analogue and aged. Briefly, I marvelled at the coalescence of all these social media forms, then read: *If you watched Baywatch followed by Gladiators then Blind Date on a Saturday evening, had 4 TV channels, started school with singing in the main hall, played in the woods, always rode your bike, a game was Kiss Chase or Bulldog with not a computer in sight, had to be in before dark, got grounded if you were late, not even the home phone was mobile,…vandalism was scratching the school desk with a compass, you recorded the top 40 off radio on tape, got 10 sweets in a 10p mix and you turned out ok, then re-post:, THIS IS WHEN BRITAIN WAS GREAT BRITAIN!!!!* I saved the tweet on its own app, then opened up Facebook and found the Memory Lane page. On Twitter, the post had engendered its own meme format. Users had begun to create their own captions – @yootywrites: 'If you circle jerked a room of people singing God Save the Queen before it got dark with a computer in sight…a game was running after a bus for 350 million quid, got a full English in your local caff for £15 and you turned out okay then re-post: THIS IS WHEN BRITAIN WAS GREAT BRITAIN!!!!' But on Facebook, a coterie of older users gave responses antiquated in their syntax, which was unstyled and sincere. In comments by the post, avatars displayed next to first and last names hung above sentences that read 'Hear hear', or 'Jemma Lane – LOL remember all this? Where have the years gone?'

At lunch, I walked to the gardens by St James's Church, sat amid the hollyhocks and bramble planted there and scrolled through the Memory Lane Facebook page for half an hour more. Some of the posts were photos or text, but more often they were illustrations – beautiful images that could have come from a children's book. In one of them, two water-coloured figures of men in bottle-green uniforms deposited the clean, virtually empty contents of large aluminium cans into the open back of a truck: the illustration was titled 'WHO REMEMBERS proper bin men'. I tried my best to recognise that the cultural identification I felt with these posts stemmed only from the fact that the touchpoints, gestures, images they referenced were things I had been handed through a screen: reruns of nineties shows and period dramas on Netflix; Instagram accounts dedicated to sixties fashion in London. When I looked up, the hollyhocks, the bramble, carefully preened, induced nostalgia for Oxford and its carefully tended-to green; for the University Parks by Bradmore Road. I swallowed hard, the impulse to miss what now felt like home, and in reality, never had been. Another notification did the work of distracting me instead: a couple of days previously, there had been a Cabinet cull. Now, a listicle did the work of synthesising who was in and who was out. I read the names of the new Home Secretary, Chancellor, Foreign Secretary. I read a list of names I did not recognise, or barely recognised: these names had resigned, been sacked, quit. The gardens churned. The smell of street food, the sound of ice cream doled out; the office workers in rotas on each bench; the mothers wiping their children's chins, the pigeons plucking discarded crusts. An email came through: HR could give me two weeks' worth of advance. I looked up from my phone at the summer recess.

II.I

The mystery of the intern's Wolseley lunches got solved one month in. On 8 August, I passed under Piccadilly's white arches and saw them at one of the restaurant's marble bars. Two in the afternoon. The stone tomb of a room. The slabs of rock and slabs of brick, all burnished. And

the intern, their amber beret; their narrow legs tangling the rails of a gold metal stool. I watched them order an espresso and waited to see whether they would have anything else. They did not.

After my conversation with the managing editor, I had doubled down on my efforts to arrive early at the office and leave late. I gave pointed waves to my colleagues whenever they left at 5 or 6 p.m., emailed updates to the team at eight at night on work finished and work to be done. The more I tried, the more coolly my efforts were received. The managing editor thanked me diligently at each emailed list, but the sign-off was always 'Kind regards' – never the initial, the treacly 'x' that punctuated the missives she sent the office at large. I wondered whether the intern, in their direct correspondence with her, was a beneficiary of such 'x's. Each morning, I watched them high-five the building's receptionist on the way into the office, hug the managing editor and wish her a happy whatever day of the week it was. I decided it was very probable she did sign off her emails to them with an 'x', but no matter how closely I watched them in the office, I could not decipher what it was they knew to pass through it with such ease; to be so universally accepted. In any case, it was impossible to ask. They had avoided me, carefully, since I had failed to reply to their invitation to the pub. On the way back from seeing them in the Wolseley, in an alcove in the Burlington Arcade, I called my mother to complain. The response was not what I wanted.

You can't start crying every time something goes wrong.

I'm not crying.

You have to learn to take things on the chin better.

I do, that's why I'm calling you. I need a place to vent that's not the office.

My mother sighed. I'd feel a lot better if I knew all these ridiculous decisions you've been making with your life were at least making you happy.

The next day I watched the intern leave a Post-it note on their screen. It said, *Off to raid the fashion cupboard for gems xxx*. They returned an hour later, wearing sunglasses and a baby-blue silk coat with a ruffled white bib; holding another, red fur one. The beauty editor shrugged on this last piece, and the picture editor grinned delightedly through her phone at the two of them as they posed for photos. Obviously I'm not keeping this one, the intern said when they had finished laughing.

But I talked the lovely bunch downstairs into letting me sell it on. I do think the red one is hot, though. Especially on you, darling.

Keep it, said the beauty editor, nodding sagely and stroking her sleeve. From my desk, I could see the managing editor smiling and shaking her head in front of her computer screen: indulgent, amused.

Come to dinner, my flatmate said. I had been watching Netflix on the sofa since Friday night. I looked up at her and she beckoned me to sit up with her right hand. The rings on it jangled lightly. It's pathetic for me, watching you here when I've got to slave away in a shop on a Sunday. My parents are a little further north. I have to go see them for a thing. They invite friends and family round for dinner once a week but they all work together and end up talking shop, it's boring. You can keep me company. Also, say you have to be home before eleven so that I can leave with you. Here – a buzz in my back pocket – I've texted you the postcode. I'll meet you on the street outside when my shift is done. Don't be late.

I had been moping; I did not necessarily want to leave. It was impossible to walk around London now. I felt in no way safe. But up sprung the great new motto of my life: never mind. I stuck some deodorant on, stole roses from the front garden of the building. I tried to be bodiless as I walked; tried to make it so that I could ignore the fact that I was moving myself through the streets. The city happened to me. There approached first a long stretch of terraced housing. It swelled, came upon me, then passed. There came pubs and ill-fitting shirts laughing in the direction of dresses that could not have given any warmth: clouds of tobacco and nicotine; a clutch of beer. Corner shops and grocery stores gave out bottles of wine, packets of crisps. Restaurants flickered – burger joints spat out their orders in four-digit code. Then the pavement pulsed where a flight of stairs sloped down and gave out neon light, and the flash of phones lined up outside it documented a prologue of sorts – a bouncer letting each bumbag and pair of platformed trainers in one by one. After that, things thinned, became uniform. Hedges sprang from the ground and wooden gates appeared. On one side, lambent windows kept crumbling brickwork beautiful: the sensibility of another age; the comfort of tenderly rolled out Persian rugs and mid-century lamps as twenty-first-century triumph. On the other, across from them, great squares of twentieth-century concrete block: flat roofs and plastic window frames, with cars parked outside and a miniature play-ground stuffed into the front gardens. In front of one of them, I was forced back to myself: my flatmate stood, phone in hand, head bent, scrolling. I tapped her shoulder.

Oh good, she said, and took me to the other side of the road, inside one of the houses done in Queen Anne revival style.

There was a coat rack by the door. A corridor perfor-ated at three distinct points: it opened up to a staircase at its end and mixed the sounds of a small lavatory, a kitchen and a living room at its centre. I left my shoes by the door and my flatmate guided me into the kitchen, where the entire back wall was taken up by glass doors. Through them, I could see a conservatory, radiant with string lights and holding a circle of people spread over cushions, garden furniture, a velvet sofa. Its woodwork was splintered white and wholly faded; inside, the ash-wood floors took on the same insubstantial quality as the glass. Even the furniture looked like it lacked weight. I hung by the kitchen door, staring at it, until a dark-haired woman looked up from her chopping board and said, Pri! My flatmate hugged her mother, who set down her knife and over her daughter's shoulder said, Call me Jane. She accepted the stolen roses and took me into her arms: when she drew back, she looked carefully at my face. I hear you've been on my daughter's sofa, she said. But I also hear you're making do. I nodded. Well, at any rate, she returned briskly to the chopping board, we'll feed you properly. Did she tell you who's here? It's work friends, mostly. Do go and say hello.

My flatmate led me to the glass house and easily found her place where the circle of guests naturally broke for her. She planted a kiss on the cheek of a greying man who smiled and said, Ray, before turning to his daughter.

You, he informed her, have arrived at just the right moment. I'm trying to defend social media in the arts. These two here – he gestured to his left at a man in a leather jacket and a woman with platinum-blonde eyebrows – think an iPhone has no place in the work of today.

Good luck, she said, accepting a wine glass. I hate it. Give me 35mm any day. They're all gallerists, she threw at me. But obviously with loaded families. To this, the circle scowled a little, and widened to accommodate me. I had to turn my body slightly to slot in. Christian makes beautiful films, my flatmate's father said, though whether for my benefit or in attempt to countermand his daughter's remark I wasn't sure. I'll be exhibiting them towards the end of the month. And Liza does portraits, exposing multiple rolls of film: all her subjects have more than one face. You might have seen her work before. They both think Instagram is the devil's scourge. What do you think, dear?

Oh don't, my flatmate groaned. Leave her alone. I brought her here because all she ever does is sulk on her own. You'll put her off ever talking to anyone ever again if you start to go on.

My flatmate's father wore an immaculately ironed shirt. I smoothed the front of my blouse. No, please, I said. I'd love to hear about everyone's work. I only used Instagram to look at other people, mostly.

The woman with platinum eyebrows looked over to me. You don't any more?

There wasn't much on it, I said. I prefer Twitter. Really, there was only one user that kind of made the app worth it, I kind of knew her. And then she stopped posting.

What were her pictures like?

A little contrived, I said, and paused. One of my legs had started dying but I was sitting between participants and the exchange of opinions was in full flow. If I moved there was a chance I would break it, and I did not have the authority to do that. The woman with platinum eyebrows had raised them triumphantly at my flatmate's father, sat next to me. You see, Ray. He shook his head, but before he could speak, I shook my leg as inconspicuously as I could and intervened. I'm not sure there was anything more contrived about them than any novel I've read, or film I've watched, I said. Whether those novels or films were better than an Instagram account is probably down to personal taste. I didn't think much of it as an app either, before I realised her pictures meant she could carry herself beyond... I trailed off, slightly unsure of what I meant, and then, because the circle was still looking at me to finish my sentence, I said, the way a good book takes you away from where you are, and as an excuse for getting the pins and needles out of my calf, shifted to pour myself a glass of wine. The blood rushed back. My flatmate's father nodded.

Well, that's bollocks if only because a good book should remind you exactly what the conditions of your life or the lives of the people around you are, in the first place. In the second, it's apples and oranges, my flatmate contributed. You're unlikely to even be talking about the same audiences.

No, no, her father interposed. I think perhaps we might actually be talking about reaching the same audiences in this case. Working with film is expensive, but everyone has a phone. Everyone does everything on their phone – read, watch. Sometimes create. Teresa, have you got your phone?

A woman resembling my flatmate's mother but with dyed red hair pulled out her phone.

Patrick?

The one who was sitting next to me duly showed his Huawei model. My flatmate looked pained; I saw her bite her tongue. Nevertheless, she turned to her father. We know you've got a phone, she said.

Yes, he said. He took over the point. You're both snobs, he said to the man in the leather jacket and the woman with platinum eyebrows, who only shrugged. If we were thirty years back, you'd be insisting on daguerreotypes. When you exalt the purity of working with the old ways, you both conveniently forget to remember these technologies were invented to spread access and ease, and were discarded only when something that provided better success in that endeavour took their place. Their value now is in how expensive their rarity and relative cumbersomeness has made them. They're markers of wealth and taste. He seemed to catch my expression out of the corner of his eye and smiled. You look like you want to say something, dear.

I had been biting my top lip. It came out from my teeth and tongue wetly. Come on, my flatmate said. It would be nice to hear you give an actual opinion for a change. Her father dipped his forefinger and thumb into his wine; flicked it across the room at her. Rude little girl – but he was smiling. Don't mind her, she takes after me. Please go on.

This was not encouraging. At my flatmate's comment, I thought of what the art director had said about me regurgitating headlines, and the memory made me less confident about the value of what I wanted to say. But everyone in the circle had turned towards me, and the uniform shift meant that, at last, I could position myself comfortably. I hedged.

I work at a magazine. Actually, it's quite a fatuous thing, but it's run on prestige and wealth and class. I was just thinking—

Quietly, my flatmate breathed, A shocking notion. Her father flicked more wine at her. Some of it went sideways and landed on my blouse. I resumed.

They venerate tradition and the past, but they use new tech to bring it into the present and make it shinier than it was. They retouched an archival page to show in the new issue week before last. They filter everything and then they share it on social media. Effectively, the use of all that new tech becomes a marker of wealth and taste, as you say.

Oh fuck the money, the man in the leather jacket said, bored. It's about the quality of the thing. And if you compare my films to the crap a consumer mag puts out, he said warningly to my flatmate's father, I'll withdraw my commission and you won't see me again.

It was as though I hadn't spoken. No one considered my point. I shrank. My flatmate's father held up his palms, into which my flatmate's mother deposited a platter of mezze. Having not noticed her advance, he fumbled – his attention veered. I tried to help him, and in shifting my position, noticed a tower of orange squares reflected in the roof of the conservatory's glass. I followed the reflection to its source – beyond the back garden, sequences of high rises; further back, the Grenfell Tower, sheathed.

I think, my flatmate's mother said softly, finding her seat and doling out food, quite apart from the fact that you value film for its flaws, in the same way people value, say, vinyl for that little muffled scratch under each song, I think she's the only one who's got a clue. Now – she smiled at me – what kept you coming back to your friend's Instagram?

She wasn't exactly my friend, I muttered, I'm not sure. I just did. But the answer sounded pitiable even to me, so I tried again: I wanted to know what would happen in her life next, and what that would look like. I paused. I wanted to know where she had been.

Quite right, my flatmate's mother said. Now let's talk about something else. I took a sip of my wine and

126

repeated the conversation back to myself, but with wittier, more profound lines where my parts were. And the mezze, and the coat rack; the conservatory and its array of mismatched chairs.

I've been thinking of doing a short loop, the man with the Huawei phone said, of blood running down Downing Street. You could project it on their walls, you know? Would you sponsor that? Would only take a few hundred quid. I'll make sure to acknowledge you. The reach on Twitter would be huge.

I excused myself to go to the bathroom.

The view directly across from the cistern was a shelf built into the wall, full of Molton Brown products. They were elegant in their semi-transparent coloured bottles, assembled in sets: shampoo and conditioner, hand soap and hand cream, bath oil and shower gel – they had names like Suede Orris or Oudh Accord. When I washed my hands and came away perfumed, refreshed, I felt like a god. I imagined what kind of a life it would be, to smell expensively of bergamot as a simple consequence of having taken a piss. My flatmate's mother found me sniffing the many rows of toiletries.

You were gone for a while, she said. I apologised, replaced the cap on the Sea Fennel body lotion. She led me to a colourless bedroom. A mirror fitted to the expanse of the west wall reflected the white sheets, white furniture and ceramics, LED lights; doubled it all and threw it back. There were two rooms. She looked at the reflected one for a moment, then fixed a vase of flowers on the nightstand according to how it looked in the glass. Please sit, she said, but I could not see how. I was wearing indigo-blue jeans. It seemed inescapable that they would stain the duvet, or the cream-coloured leather on the chair in front of the vanity table. I could have tied my cardigan around my waist, but still I would have worried about disordering the bed, or leaving a dent in the seat whose cushion rose so perfectly upwards. I stayed where I was. She herself remained standing and looked steadily at me.

It's not too hard on that sofa? My daughter can be very untidy.

It's fine, I said. It's okay. It's fine.

Are you sure? If I were your mother, I'd be insisting you come home immediately.

Yes. Mine is.

My flatmate's mother tipped her head. So why don't you?

I just— I gasped, and broke. Everything came in great, juddering breaths. I probably should. I don't know what I'm going to do because I don't have a contract and I thought it would be better if I left academia and got a real-world job and I thought I'd end up with a salary and a flat, and that I would have friends and a life, but when I'm not in the office I spend all my time alone and worrying about whether they'll want to keep me, and I'm really fucking sick of not having a room of my own, and sleeping on a sofa, I mean, I know I'm not homeless and there are bigger problems in the world, and you're right, I can go and stay with my parents for a bit if I have to, but why should I, when did it become ridiculous to think that a stable economy and a fair housing market were reasonable expectations? I really think growing up in the middle of a financial crash traumatised a lot of my generation and skewed our perception of what we're allowed to ask for. You know?

At this point I couldn't see for clumps of running mascara. I felt ridiculous almost as soon as my mouth closed. My flatmate's mother disappeared from my line of sight briefly, then returned with tissues. I blew my nose and did my best to stop crying. I tried to laugh instead and gestured at my own ridiculousness.

Something about your generation I've noticed, she said not unkindly once I had fallen silent, is that you give up very easily. You seem to expect things to turn out perfectly at first try. I had to work very hard – she looked briefly at the mirror – to end up in this house.

I'm not saying I don't want to work hard, I said, stung. I *do* work very hard.

No, no, I didn't mean to imply otherwise, she said at once, laying a hand on my arm. I just meant that I see a lot of people your age expecting far more than we ever did, and on a much quicker timeline. Even though you've got so much more of an advantage than I ever did. I think it might be because of how freely available the image of a glamorous lifestyle is on your phones now. I catch a glimpse of Priscilla's phone now and again over her shoulder, and you all seem to be very adept at making your lives look far more interesting than they have any right to be. The truth is, most days are inexhaustibly dull and full of striving. I did my share of boring, low-wage administrative jobs and living in bedsits, or on friends' floors as well. I'm sure your peers do, too, they just don't post about it. And then, because of a few get-rich-quick success stories, and the lack of representation around how much work it usually *does* take to attain any kind of achievement, a sort of entitlement gets bred.

That might be true, I conceded. But I didn't really mean that. I don't want anything glamorous, I just want normal things. At least you didn't feel deranged for thinking you might afford a house one day.

Honestly, she said, I didn't think about it. I rented run-down flats with friends for years. My husband and I scraped to buy the first house we did because we wanted Priscilla to have a nice room. I think until she came along, I sort of...waited to see how things would turn out.

I don't think I can do that, I whispered.

She cocked her head. Why?

I looked at my feet. You have a very beautiful home, I said finally. I think you should have been able to go through the early stages of your adulthood secure in the knowledge you would end up in it.

When I looked up, my flatmate's mother seemed to have exhaled. Her body softened. There's a face wash in the bathroom, petal, she said. You can clean that make-up off a little. When you feel better, come downstairs and have some food and wine. She led me to an en suite, where on the sink was another bottle from Molton Brown. I lathered my face and tried not to think beyond the smell of mandarin and clary sage. Back downstairs, the others had split to form several, smaller groups which talked among themselves: the only available seat was next to the man who had pulled out the Huawei phone. I smiled briefly at him and felt self-conscious at my newly bare face. He smiled back: we rocked, very slightly, towards and away from each other, each taking small repositories of breath – the pause for thought before a conversation stretched out for eternity until my embarrassment overtook me, and I made my confession: I'm not very good with names. I forgot it again as soon as he told me.

The next morning on the way into work I stopped by Regent Street, where Molton Brown had a boutique, and forgoing all thought of lunch for a few days, bought the Mandarin & Clary Sage face wash for myself.

Out on the square in front of the office, the builders had unionised. This came as a shock to all of us because none of us had ever considered that they may have felt any kind of discontent. Beyond the cigarette breaks and shouted banter we observed in passing, we knew nothing of their circumstances, only that one morning, dozens of them – far more than I would have guessed – were suddenly marching up and down the thoroughfare and abandoning their drills. From my window, I could see the scurrying of miniature neon jackets, holding banners and shouting.

Oh, the intern breathed in the same tone they used to show the office cat videos. They look so funny.

They're going to disturb the tents, the art director said, without looking up from her screen.

What? I asked.

Her eyes did not flicker from the screen. They're going to disturb the homeless in the garden outside, someone should tell them.

I did not understand what she meant until I did a coffee run, and on my way back, the combined effects of the strike and the torn-up walkway forced me onto the green. While I'd been gone, the protest had circled back to the front of the square, but it had not interrupted the ordinances of those on their lunch break. The builders could usually have been found reclining alongside various office workers anyway, and I could easily picture myself, in two hours, doing exactly what those eating triangle sandwiches were doing now: headphones in, neck bent towards a screen or a book, or else just the grass.

I balanced the coffees in their cardboard tray. Rather than tangle myself up in the crowd again, I walked the perimeter of the garden towards the back gate. Near it, a row of muddy blue tents lined up with their backs to the curlicue iron railing. A German shepherd burrowed its nose disconsolately into the grass. It whined. Once I was aware of it, it was impossible to unhear – to the sound of protesting builders I now added a high-pitched whistle.

I had been working at the magazine for a month. How had I not noticed this before? Claustrophobia began to set in. I wanted to get back to the benign white wood of my desk, but that impulse was the very thing I was trying to cull in myself. I felt my breathing increase. The tents had not been there in July, I was sure, but I had not noticed their arrival either. How long had I been negligent for? There was chaos in the square's garden, and I, trying to recover my equilibrium, gripped the coffees, swayed lightly where I stood until a man in jeans and a white T-shirt asked me whether I was okay. I nodded. I wanted to ask whether there was anything I could do for him, but he was the one who gave me a pat on the back, asked whether I would like some water. When I shook my head, he retreated; sat in front of one of the tents and tipped the bottle he was holding towards the mouth of the fatigued beast instead, massaging its flanks. I ran back towards the office.

Oh, good, the associate editor said, accepting her matcha. Look, listen, you're young. Tell me if you recognise this at all. She fumbled with her phone until some sound began to play from it, much too low to hear. I hummed perfunctorily while she jabbed the screen.

You know, it might have just passed you by, or it might not have, but I want to see whether you like it even if you haven't heard it, you know?

I had never seen someone have so much trouble with their phone. The sound jerked up and down: I strained for a few guitar chords – they pulled back into the phone's speakers and then dispensed again, breaking the air-conditioned calm of the office. Once I recognised the song, I frowned.

You see, it was quite popular in the nineties, the associate editor said, not looking at me, but at the row of holes at the bottom of her phone, as though she could see the sound coming out of it. He was a total heart-throb. Not that he lived up to his image in person, you know, but then I met him not long after his wife left him and he was saddled with this baby he had absolutely no clue what to do with, and the baby had the same name as the wife, which really couldn't have been helpful. No idea why he named the child that. I imagine he never did get therapy for the whole ordeal, he probably thought writing this song when she left him was enough. And of course, I was there to help him—

I love this song, the features editor said.

Yes, me too. It was always best to hear it in person, of course, this is terrible. He used to sing it to me, which I didn't *quite* appreciate, you know, him singing a song about his ex-wife to me, while we were... Well, anyway, the point is – she looked up from the phone, suddenly focused – his wife was quite beautiful. After she left him, she circled around society for a bit, and she graced our pages a handful of times. Now, of course, there's this nostalgia for the nineties with the younger generation and what have you, I've heard this song quite a bit. His daughter's agreed to do a fashion shoot for us and we'll dress her up in McQueen and vintage Galliano and whatever else – it's quite clever, no? The whole thing about finding fame the song talks about: we're going to style her as this nineties starlet. She's a lovely little thing. She looks so much like her mother: we've emulated a lot of the looks she was wearing in the back issues for this. It's good, it'll work for older readers, and it'll tap into all those girls like you. Anyway, do you know the song?

Yes, I said. I was back on South Parks Road in Oxford; I was in my thin red dress, holding a bottle of champagne. I was googling Ghislane's name. The smell of cut grass.

It's fabulous, isn't it?

Yes.

The last time I'd worn the dress had been the night of the parties held by the English faculty and my neighbour's college. It had been tossed into a carrier bag for the charity shop when I was getting rid of my things during the last days of my teaching post. I wanted it back.

She hit pause on her phone. The sound stopped. When you've done all the page furniture and you've put in all the details, run it past me. I don't want her father calling me at all hours, he's less interesting than he used to be.

Yes, I said. Are you still living in the Berkeley?

No, she groused, once more absorbed in her phone. I'm doing Claridge's now. Make the Thames Water bastards pay.

The strike action outside the office and around the square took a day to resolve itself – or at least, by the following morning, the square was empty. There was no one to hose down the fine layer of dust that spread over the remaining pavement, nearby windows, the grass and blue tents. The square had acquired a ghoulish, chalky calm which regular passers-by seemed to revel in: the absence of drills, of shouted Polish or cockney, more room in the thoroughfare for pedestrians to flit between each bus and car. The place was demolished, but more women than ever flocked towards the revolving doors, holding magazines and shopping bags while they posed for photos. The quiet stretched out for a week. Into this, the photos of Ghislane came, with an accompanying list detailing the items she wore, where they came from, and how much they cost.

Have you read this? the picture editor volleyed over her iMac, holding up a forest-green book with pink lettering. It's great. It's like this manifesto for women who want to succeed, but it completely turns the idea on its head. It's not prescriptive: 'this is how you get the good life', bit by bit. It's more about life not being linear, self-care, reasonable goals, and feeling accomplished in yourself without external validation. The author says success is *innate*, it's always there, in the person you are, not outside you in the arbitrary things you want to achieve. She's really honest in it, she talks a lot about her personal privilege and all her ups and downs. I think you'd like it.

I grimaced; looked, instead, at my screen. The opening shot was of Ghislane against an olive background, in a thin leather bralette and an equally thin matching pencil skirt. Someone had slicked her hair into one uniform ponytail: two front pieces of hair curtained her face in an artful curve; her make-up was calculatedly bare, save for a brickish-red smear of lipstick. She had been shot twisting a white banner around her body onto which someone had scrawled in deliberately jagged text *YES TO THE REVOLUTION*.

I thought she was going to be shot in context of her dad's song? I frowned.

The picture editor walked round to look at the photos. Yeah, she didn't like the association. It's a shame, I love that song. But she said she wanted something more in tune with how women want to be portrayed today, and something about existing in her own right.

It's a protest photoshoot? I could not stymie my incredulity.

Yeah. You should have seen the stroke she gave wardrobe, insisting on a last-minute change to the entire concept. Actually, she gave everyone a stroke, we almost didn't get His Majesty's approval on it. But I like it, the picture editor said, cocking her head as though a new angle would impart a sense of profundity on Ghislane's stomach, peeking out from between the white sheet and leather clothes. It's a laugh after all that calamity we had going on with the builders yesterday.

Plus it's better than the usual high couture bollocks. She looks very sexy. They made a point of making sure the photographer was a woman, and it was the photographer who came up with the banners, actually, because she wanted her to feel powerful – I think there was a whole conversation about encouraging a sense of play and autonomy with how she was using the props. Empowerment, and all that. Anyway, this book, I finished it last night and—

I titled the page 'Exist to Resist' and moved to the next image. I thought about myself, walking in circles around my room in Bradmore Road, reading bits of Pater in order to make sense of Ghislane's Instagram. Nothing had changed. Now it was Ghislane on an InDesign document, against an olive background, wearing a silvery, sheer slip dress, waving a white flag, and me inputting text to make sense of her. I typed: *Sheer satin slip dress, stylist's own.* Now it was her, in low-slung trousers and a halter neck, ready to be sent to print. I typed: *Rage against the machine.* Now, she had Chanel Rouge Noir on her nails and two thin braids on either side of her face. I made to stick more nonsense words in and came up short. Do the words even matter? I murmured absently. Does anyone read them?

Try 'The future is female', the picture editor said. I typed it in. Before I got to the 'm' in 'female' the script disappeared off the page. Oh, it doesn't fit, she said, and I could hear she was disappointed. Anyway, she continued, have you read it? The author's coming for a talk next month and I think I'm going to go. You might be interested, too.

I stared at the screen.

I knew her, I said finally. Then corrected myself – That's not true, I didn't *know* her, but she was around when I was a research assistant.

At Oxford?

Yes.

You never talk about your old job. Do you miss it?

I miss the place. I miss the town. Or belonging to it. I'm not sure what it would be like to go back now. None of my things are there. I reflected. None of my things are here, either.

Unusually for the magazine, in some of the pictures Ghislane was smiling. In one, she was bent forward with her hands on her knees, mid-laughter. The picture editor tapped the screen. What about her? A few people here know her dad, and they say he's a real relic. She seems very *now*, though, doesn't she? She's been doing interviews here and there and she makes it look so easy; all these young girls do. I suppose it feels like she's been around forever because of her dad's song, though, which must be hard. But she's got the whole activist, low-key fashion plate, not really fixed in one area, doing loads of stuff at one time thing going on. My daughter's a few years younger than you both and she says she's going to have a career like that. Did Ghislane do that sort of stuff when you knew her?

I don't know. She was on Instagram a lot, I sighed. Actually, she looked nothing like how she does in these photos. She was someone else to me then. She was a student. I felt superior to her. It wasn't even that long ago.

I couldn't say any more.

We tried tracking her social media presence, the picture editor said awkwardly, she's doing this thing where she archives each of her photos before the next one goes up. So we have to get it all from second-hand sources and little fan accounts. It doesn't make us look great when we have to credit it. Could you reach out to her?

I shifted uneasily, and the picture editor nodded. It's really easy to fall out of touch now, isn't it? Although when I think about it, it's not any more common than it used to be, there's just less of an excuse now. Everyone takes offence more readily if you leave them on read.

Ghislane's face pouted at me from the screen. The only yellow boxes the art director had put in were on the background, indicating where lighting and tone should be fixed; stray cables taken out. I'll try emailing her, I said, then looked at the green-and-pink book still on the picture editor's desk. I read that in June. I don't know how much it did for me.

I walked round so that I could look at the inside cover, where a well-lit photo of the author, young, athletic, tawny, adorned the tasteful heavy jacketing. I flicked through it and remembered what it was about the book that had irked me so much. It was easy, I had said to my flatmate in June, to envision the idea of success as innate when nothing in the set-up of your life would ever allow you to fall short of a good one. The author had been financially comfortable since birth; now owned London property; was conventionally beautiful, and expensively educated. She suffered the occasional wobble in her mental health, but then, who didn't? I could not inherently fault her for any of these things. But the idea of her profiting from having written a book about how to attain something she had never had to work for upset me, still.

The picture editor watched me turn the pages in silence, confused. I gave her a good-humoured shrug. On my way back to my desk, I caught sight of the intern, eating cashews and squinting at something in front of them. Somehow, perhaps because of the mop of blonde curls on their head, the effect was cherubic. When the beauty editor, at the desk across from them, caught their eye, they grinned before resuming their work.

Actually, I said, I would like to go to that talk.

You said it didn't do anything for you, the picture editor laughed. I forced myself to smile.

I probably read it in too much of a rush the first time. I'll try it again.

She looked unconvinced.

After the stainless white of my flatmate's parents' house, the building in which she lived yellowed further in my eyes. When, one working week on from their dinner, on Friday, I walked from the office to Barons Court, the sweat that had accumulated under my arms, that had made the gap between my sandals and my feet slippery and coiled into my hair, made the empty, aged dirtiness of the lobby even more manifest. I had taken ten minutes to lie on a patch of grass in Hyde Park and remained itchy while walking up the stairs; putting the key into the door; turning it; letting myself in. I saw, scribbled and left on the mantelpiece: *Back Sunday night*. I began to breathe a little more freely, until I went to take a shower. My flatmate had neglected the cleaning rota and the bathroom floor looked filthier than I was. I rose, on instinct, to tread it on tiptoe, and resigned myself to the dry chalk of rubber gloves and dull bleach headache. By the time I was able to shower my muscles ached and nothing felt right – hot water seemed only to make me sweat more, to make things worse; cold water was uncomfortable, did nothing to shift the layer of grime I felt prickling into my skin. Everything was wrong. I finished washing and went to her bed, dragged myself into it, did not come out until Sunday afternoon. I did nothing, except occasionally use the toilet or eat. My phone illuminated every so often on the pillow next to me – flashed news updates, the date, the time: kept me somewhat in the world. When my flatmate was due back, I took another shower; massaged my face with the Molton Brown clary sage wash.

Over the weekend, her bedroom had induced an odd sense of pity in me. It was furnished with the same cheap wood the landlord had left in the living room and light, ineffectual curtains, but she had gone to great lengths to inject some glamour. Heavy cardboard bags from Selfridges and Liberty were arranged by the mirror, all of them empty. The wardrobe had been wrapped in fairy lights; there was a table covered in MAC cosmetics and scented candles. Like her mother, my flatmate had pushed the bed to the centre of the back wall opposite the door so that it dominated the room. Everything else was in orbit around it. There were table mirrors propped up on nearly every available flat space, though with less elegance than I had seen in her mother's house the previous weekend: Polaroid photos and small potted plants surrounded them. I made the bed and stacked up one frilly cushion on top of the next. My flatmate was in her late twenties, but I could picture what she must have been like as a teenager by her room. I let myself out;

crossed the two steps between the corridor and the kitchen, which was littered with its usual jewellery-making tools and sparse, unsentimental array of pasta, store-bought pesto, a cheap plastic kettle. I might have crossed into a different flat. I felt quite tenderly towards her when she returned.

You look like shit, she informed me. Here, come help.

The tenderness disappeared. She was dragging a cluster of reusable bags. They bulged by her knees. I took four from her.

What's all this?

Tins.

Tins?

I could feel her irritation. Yes, tins. The kitchen was small enough to make the floor an island of Waitrose plastic. I stepped gingerly around the green.

Tins of what?

She pulled out chopped tomatoes, chickpeas, soup. Do you know what, she mused, we could actually stack them on the open shelves, they're so kitsch they're almost aesthetic. The tins began to go up in pyramids against the kitchen's dirty blue walls. Grudgingly, I allowed that the combination of precious metals and gems on the countertops against the delicate illustrations of tuna, the syrup and peaches, the white sans-serif HEINZ logo on duck-egg blue, was quite evocative.

You could print a few pictures of Warhol, I mused. Find some really nice frames and prop them up against all this.

That might be taking the piss, my flatmate said, leaning back from her iPhone and taking a photo of the finished shelf. I mean, these are doomsday measures in the end. She bit the inside of her cheek and tried a square crop.

I'm sorry, what?

She began to filter one of the photos. Yellowhammer leak? All over the papers this morning? The idiocy of our government will kill us all? Hello? Do you not read the news? I raised my eyebrows until she noticed. I'm not *posting* this, she said defensively. It's just for memories a few years down the line. She looked briefly at the stacked shelf. And I'm not stupid, I'm only half serious. But better safe than sorry. Austerity has been bad enough these past few years anyway. Anyway, if you eat a tin, replace a tin, okay?

I began snatching up the bags she had left littered on the floor, folding them with exaggerated pointedness. You forgot to clean the bathroom, I said. It's not a big deal but I ended up having to do it after I got home from work stressed.

She was unmoved; adjusted a tin of Ambrosia Devon custard so that the blue-and-white house in the middle of the field lined up dead centre with the tin below it. Eventually, I heard her blow out a, Sorry, and as she passed on her way out a murmured, It's my bloody bathroom anyway.

After she had gone into her bedroom, I took the sheets from the drawer they had been stuffed in at the beginning of summer: set them to wash on a warm, gentle cycle with plenty of fabric softener, and then stretched them across a drying rack so that they filled the living room. I gathered my own bundle of possessions out of my suitcase and arranged them in and around the cabinet drawers – a small stack of books, my toiletry bag, my clothes. When the sheets were dry, I ironed them so that they patterned in squares: each crease brought up crisp, uniform tents. I tucked and spread until the slump of the sofa was obscured by cotton, plumped the pillows at one end and smoothed a thin blanket down just below them. I set my bag down and lined up my two pairs of shoes on the floor at the opposite end of the pillows, and in the morning, I did not dismantle my bed. I made it up perfectly, left a couple of books arranged neatly on it, and dared anyone disturb what I had made for myself.

On 26 August, I had to ask whether I still had a job.

I had been DMing Ghislane. Instagram. I was days into the process and had finally managed as far as *Dear Ghi*, before an automated email lit up at the top of my phone and informed me that my IT contract was due to expire unless renewed by my line manager. I had been receiving these emails daily: we had started at fourteen days, gone to ten, down to nine, and now the perfectly round number of a week.

It was one of the rare days that the Editor was in. I saw the managing editor taking him through the coming issue's flatplan; him, eyeing a croissant she had left untouched on her desk. There are more around the corner, she told him, and he declined. He was working on losing what he called his 'relaunch paunch'; a year's worth of breakfasts at Claridge's: the hard work of rehabilitating the image of the magazine. I waited until he had retreated into his office and approached.

Why don't we regroup? the managing director smiled once I had stuttered my way to the point. I'll get back to you with availability. We can talk about how you're getting on. How does that sound?

It sounded terrible. I smiled back and said thank you.

After this, the message to Ghislane wrote itself in minutes. It said, *you probably don't remember me*; and, *the photos are *so* empowering and strong*; and *really good to see you've landed on your feet so quickly*; and *was wondering if I could put you in touch with the picture editor here for some usable personal shots*; and *would love to hear how you've been more generally; maybe have lunch? Warm wishes –*

I sent it without reading it back.

Eventually, September stuffed, inflated itself into the air, and when the rain came, it was not with any commitment or delight.

Because of how consistently it rained, everything stayed green. August was still fresh enough that I could wish it back from the previous week; could ease out a thousand different ways to spend my body no longer possible. I had been waiting for a flat of my own; I had been waiting for my life, as I wanted it. To go wild swimming in the ponds in Hampstead; to shop for fistfuls of cheap vine-ripened tomatoes and cook them in the evenings with a glass of red wine. To wear thin, gauzy white; read, and eat Cornish ice cream. To have hot, hazy evenings in a cinema or a cafe, and then the last few hours of daylight in garden squares, stretched out in dwindling sun. But it was September now. Days shortened, went cold. When my phone dispensed photos from the House of Commons of an MP lounging across the bench, for an unwitting moment I felt seen, before I remembered to apply context and become morally outraged.

The true form of things was the office, now oddly luminescent in its whiteness against the gradually greying weather; the sudden appearance of dun-coloured coats and jumpers. My contract, extended for two more months. The managing editor, earnest: After that, your probation period will be up and I don't think we'll be moving forward, but we're so proud of how much you've grown. I'm sure you'll have no trouble finding something else.

I felt nothing. Earlier that day, the senior editor had boomed over his desk: News? And the features team: Twenty-one MPs had the whip removed. To which the senior editor shook his head – We can't do anything sexy with that.

It took two weeks for Ghislane to respond. Each time my phone gave out the descending tone that signalled a notification, my heart did a corresponding drop. When, on 9 September, I saw her name beneath the grey banner, I flipped my phone over so violently it dropped to the floor. I left it there for twenty minutes until the art director came back from her lunch break and put it back on my desk.

Oh, your screen will want fixing. Did that happen just now? What's that from Ghislane?

The picture editor perked up opposite me. You emailed her?

I swallowed. No, direct messaged. Er – I tapped gingerly around splinters – she says...Thanks for getting in touch. Please forward this address to your picture editor. Smiley face. I read out the email address she had provided. I stared at my phone. There was nothing on my Instagram – no profile picture or posts. Only my username. It was likely she had, in fact, forgotten who I was. The picture editor asked me to repeat the address so that she could write it down, and so I read the message out again, all two lines of it, and felt my mouth go numb.

Very good of her, the art director said to the picture editor.

Yes, she seems the sort.

I could feel the spit pooling under my tongue. They waited for me to agree.

By the time Parliament was prorogued, I could not delude any of the drudgery of my work into the beauty of summer days. The builders had come back with their accompanying din: bits of the pavement returned, looking no different to what they had been before, and construction work began in the reception area of the building itself, prompting the associate editor into a feral hysteria. It rained incessantly. Public transport was sodden with it, and packed; I kept losing umbrellas, my shoes soaked through, my books wrinkled, my coat began to smell. I started and ended most of my days wet. For all of this I should have spent the month screaming, but the intern's cheerful face when they walked in each morning kept my voice low. I cried frequently on the sofa.

The picture editor made good on her suggestion to attend the talk on success. I followed her into the building's first-floor boardroom, where folding chairs had been locked into perfect rows and tables pushed against the perimeter. On each of them, pyramids of the speaker's book were stacked now towards the front of the table, now back, so that vases of flowers and complimentary mugs with a Beckett quote on them wove between. The intern was there, exchanging ten-pound notes for a copy of the book and a customary penny. There was an admirable smoothness to the way their hands switched between the cash-box and each book dispensed. I watched them. They smiled perfunctorily at me.

I sat in the front row and regretted it. The speaker was luminously beautiful, raised slightly above us on a bar stool. Despite how much I had come to hate her book, it was impossible not to like her. She spoke with enthusiasm and open sincerity: she asked for the opinions and questions of the room with a genuine belief that knowing them was the key to becoming a better person.

I want this to be more of a conversation than a talk, if that's all right, she said, tucking strands of hair behind her ears. Because I think we all have very different measures for what constitutes a success story and I don't necessarily feel I have a right to sit and preach to you about how I've achieved my own. Often, the very insecurities we have about ourselves are the things other people admire about us. I know that every time I look at a woman telling me about all the things she thinks she's done wrong in life, a part of me starts despairing and thinking, *But you're perfect*. At the same time, she said warningly, although it's important to acknowledge that impulse, I always try to turn the volume down on it. It's impossible to know another person's pain, and I really feel no one has a right to judge anyone else. Particularly women. I think men already spend enough of their time judging us, so why would we make it any easier on them? Let's all just make a commitment to try to be kind to each other in this room, and to keep being kind even after we've left it. So. Would anyone like to kick us off?

There was a silence, a shuffling around the room, and then eventually someone spoke up and said, I really liked how in your book, you talked about your thirties not being at all like how you thought they'd be, and that it was liberating to let that image of yourself go in your forties. I was just wondering whether you still keep any kind of life goals for yourself generally, or whether you've completely given up on that as a concept.

The speaker laughed. Um, so I don't want to be presumptuous in thinking that you've all read the book, she said. So I'll quickly explain. I got married in my late twenties and I thought my thirties would basically look like a fifties sitcom, or a nineties one at least, where I'd stay with my husband, we'd buy a house, I'd experience some kind of career progression – and also, I'd written a book that I thought I'd publish and acquire a glowing reputation as a famous novelist. She made sure to laugh at herself. But midway through my thirties, my husband divorced me because I didn't want children, which actually upset some conservatively minded people in my life who I thought I was quite close with. I got fired from my job, and I was told on no less than twenty-six occasions that my novel wasn't really much good. Essentially, every system and mechanism I'd used to check in on myself with and see whether I was 'doing' life right fell apart, and I had to learn to feel a sense of accomplishment and seek rewards from something other than a relationship, or a job, or material wealth, or any of the other usual stuff we're told will make us happy but which actually keeps us in the grip of the patriarchy.

The room clucked sympathetically.

Happiness is something you decide for yourself, she continued. And everyone gets there in the end. I've just bought a house with my boyfriend, but will I marry him? Not sure. I don't think either of us needs the conventional institution of marriage to make each other happy. We can be together and happy for the rest of our lives in our own way. We have a *partnership*. The main thing has been shifting my attitude so that my personal and professional success is now a thing I think of as innately within me, and achievable at any given moment. It's been very liberating. I don't judge myself by anyone else's standards any more. She manufactured a pause by gathering her well-cut hair into a low-slung bun and adjusted her trousers so that the seam ran down her leg in a straight line. Then she addressed the person who had asked the first question.

Do I still keep any life goals for myself? the speaker mused, looking towards the ceiling. She tapped her heel against her stool. I mean, yes, she said finally. I think that's important in that it provides me with a sense of discipline. They can be as small as – I will walk the dog today, or I will write however many pages. And then I'll let myself eat a tub of hummus as a reward. The room laughed. But in a grander scheme, not really, I guess, not any more. I keep a set of basic principles for myself, like, try not to be a dick, don't intentionally hurt anyone, shop sustainably. And the rest...what will be will be. But I think, if you *do* want to keep life goals for yourself, she added, that's fine. Maybe just be flexible with them, you know? If you don't get there by a certain age, just push the deadline back a little. And decide what those goals will add to your life. Because, okay, a life goal of raising happy kids, or feeling empowered is great. But losing those extra ten pounds or learning that language just so that you can be a more perfect accoutrement for a society that won't even value your skills and literally makes money off your self-doubt is crazy.

There was a round of applause. I put my hands together lightly.

Another hand went up. Could you talk a little more about the tyranny of looking perfect and being perfect? a perfectly beautiful woman asked. Especially in a social sense? For example, I love the bit in your book where you say that feminism should only be used to empower other women rather than to put them down.

That was a quote, the speaker said, nodding. A very wise one, I think. Yes. I think it's okay for us all to make mistakes and to be a bit messy, and to sometimes miss the mark. We're all human. I think the internet has made it very difficult to be a nuanced, complicated, authentic self.

Don't you think, I heard myself saying, and hating it, that it's important to be held accountable if what you're doing is wrong? For example, a lot of feminism has been co-opted into a marketable luxury, or made to seem like a club whose membership is dictated by unequal wealth distribution and unequal beauty standards. It's no longer just a basic premise for society to try and adjust itself to and function on, like...I searched my brain. The weather, I finished lamely.

Someone coughed. The room began to shrink down on me. The speaker continued smiling at me, as though expecting me to go on, and so I did. What would you say to women who have used feminism as a 'brand' to market diet products, thousand-dollar T-shirts and exclusive club memberships with?

The sun seemed to radiate out of the speaker's face. She remained utterly calm, taking time to select her words with care. I would say even feminists sometimes fail at feminism, she said finally. And yes, it's very important that we examine any hypocrisy within the movement. That being said, I think it's also crucial to remember that we don't live in a utopia where feminism can gain importance and thrive if it isn't propped up by the major frameworks in modern-day society – and for the time being, one of those is a market economy.

But – this came out desperately, I struggled to adjust the pitch of my voice to her cool, her calm – surely the goal of the movement is to prop up major frameworks in society, rather than to be propped up by them?

Well, sure, the speaker said. But it's a journey, right? First you infiltrate them. Then you spark a revolution from within. Then world domination. She winked. The room laughed. Thank you. The speaker smiled at me. That was a very interesting point. I smiled back and felt like a toad assaulting a princess; wanted desperately to go back in time and clamp my mouth shut. I felt judged by the women in the audience around me; I felt that it would reflect better on my character if the speaker, with her reasonableness, with her constant niceness and luminous skin, liked me.

What would you say the best way to cope with failure is? someone else asked.

Um, breathe, the speaker said. Do whatever you need to do to get through it. Yoga? Do it. Packet of digestives? Eat it. Ignore calls for a week? It's your right. Do it knowing that it's temporary, and tomorrow is another day.

What's the best thing writing this book has taught you? I asked, wanting desperately to save face.

That's an excellent question, she beamed. I think that everything is relative. As I've been doing this tour, I've listened to a lot of people talk about their lives, and definitely the best thing it's taught me is a kind of self-awareness. For example, before writing this book, I think I was blind to a lot of the structural privilege in my life. You know, I had fairly middle-class parents, and I went to boarding school, and I'm a thin, white woman. All of that, I gradually understood and came to terms with, and now I definitely want to use my voice to help lift others, if that's in my power. But I think, also, the best people I've spoken to know that even when you're successful, pain is pain, no matter how it happens, or who it happens to. You know, heartbreak is heartbreak. Loss is loss. We all just need to support each other and love each other.

There was another round of applause.

Okay, I think that's enough of me up here, she said. Um, I'll be at the back of the room signing copies of the book if anyone wants one, or if you just want a chat, that's fine too. I just want to close with a quote from Carl Jung, which I have actually had printed on this T-shirt, she said winking at me and opening her blazer briefly. I am not what happened to me, she read out, I am what I choose to become.

On my way out, I knocked one of the Beckett mugs into my bag and placed it visibly on top of one of the first-floor bins.

The iMac screen flashed new copy at me when I got back to my desk. I printed the page.

What is it?

The art director raised an eyebrow. Climate protests are sexy.

And where are the photos?

Non-existent. We've pulled some sustainable couture for the society protesters to march in, we're shooting them wearing it – the art director raised her hands and made exaggerated air quotes – in the streets, as it were.

How can couture be sustainable?

It's made for life.

Yes, but who actually wears it in real life?

The art director tapped her fingers to her temple and rolled her eyes. I tried again.

What's with all the protests in this issue?

Rehabilitation. The great and the good of society with a capital 's' can no longer survive as good-looking laya-bouts. There are enough name-drops in that article to sink a yacht, she grinned.

I began to read out loud from the sheets. When the strikes are happening, it's never about apportioning blame, says one privately educated, Oxbridge grad. Attendees look for systemic rather than personal change, and remain unflustered by allegations of hypocrisy. We're all guilty. Most of us, whether we come to these protests or not, drive cars, or buy single-use plastic, that kind of thing, she shrugs. If you exist on planet Earth, you're part of the problem. I stopped reading and looked up. The art director was stifling a series of snorts.

Do read the bit, she said, where they list the aristocrats, celebrities and royals who have donated to the cause.

I scanned further down the page until the words 'envi-ronmentalist banker' caught my eye. I read aloud again: It's a paradox for a lot of people, but I dispute that, he says. You can't convict someone for making money. Money is neutral. It's what you do with it that counts.

I stopped reading. Money is not neutral, I said finally. How you earn it is just as important as how you spend it. I tried to say more, but my mouth fell open, huffing, useless. The art director, taking in the look on my face, began laughing openly.

If you're so disgusted with it, my flatmate said in the kitchen later that evening once I had read the article to her, why don't you go and protest yourself?

It's different for me, I said. I'm not white. Getting arrested means something different.

She did not look up from the ring she was filing. Have you ever been unfairly targeted by law enforcement before in your life?

No, I said awkwardly. And I don't plan on it.

Sounds like a cop-out to me, she said. Between your accent and the way you dress, I doubt you're any more likely to be targeted than I am.

I dress that way for work. And you don't know that. Why are you so determined to be discriminated against? You've never expressed any kind of strong alliance or BAME concern before – you're entirely the product of an educated, socially mobile middle class. You were born in the last of the blind glory days. It's Gen Z who have it rough, not you. You're one of Blair's babies.

I'm not, I said, shocked. You should see what it's like in the office. One of my colleagues is this rich, typically English-looking girl – she's not even that good-looking, she looks like a chipmunk. She's terrible at her job. But she's treated like a daughter by everyone because she has perfect skin, and fits sample size.

155

Yes, it must be tragic for you as a mere size 8 in Levi's, my flatmate said drily. Having left a cushy job in Oxford and arrived to discover you can't be accepted by a society magazine.

That's not what I meant. I'm not looking to be accepted by them, I just think it's bollocks that she's more rewarded than I am because she was born one of them.

I know what you meant. No offence though, it's getting boring hearing you whine about your job while you remain completely oblivious to your own privilege. And having finished the ring, she slipped it onto her finger and held it up to the light. Then she turned her hand to show the gem to me. Can you tell it's fake?

I looked closely at the ring. Its colour was blood orange and bitter. I shook my head. My flatmate nodded. Good. Right. By the way, you owe me £58 for bills and council tax.

Sure, I said.

And another thing. She began washing her hands. I was wondering if you wouldn't mind taking the sheets off the sofa in the morning like you used to? And putting your stuff away when you're not home? It's just that when I work from home, I need the living room.

You make most of your jewellery in the kitchen, I pointed out.

Yes, but I do admin in the living room, she said. Tidy room, tidy mind. Can we keep it tidy, please?

I looked at the chaos in the kitchen: the thin layer of metal filings and dust on the floor and inching towards the kitchen knives. Plastic baggies full of gemstones jostled with the cutting boards, the sink stacked full with cups of greying, milky tea. I thought about the bathroom as I regularly found it, uncleaned and laced with her hair, and as I did so, my eyes moving down, saw that the side of my jeans had been blackened by the dust on the kitchen countertop. Across the corridor, I could see the door to my flatmate's bedroom firmly closed to the dirt produced by every ring she made. I remembered the twee Polaroid photos, fairy lights and cacti, all dustless; felt a rising irritation. Tidy like the kitchen you keep messing up, or the bathroom you never clean? I asked idly. Her eyes narrowed, but she did not shout. Instead she looked levelly at me.

Did you sleep in my room?

Sorry?

When I was gone for the weekend, I got back and my pillow smelt like your shampoo.

The room went hot; shrank, receded. There was my heartbeat, in my ears; I could hear it making everything small and loud. When I shook my head, I felt like a child. My flatmate narrowed her eyes further.

Right. Just keep your stuff packed up and out of my way when you're in my flat, okay?

Because a kind of cold war had broken out after the scene in the kitchen, I found any excuse not to come home during sociable hours. I continued going into the office early and staying late. I bought cheap cinema tickets, or nursed a coffee for four hours in a cafe and sat bored over a book. At one point, I did go to the ladies' pond; sat on the banks and admired the magpies darting blue-tailed around them, then grew bored of that as well: I had no inclination to swim in the cold or to get mud in my hair, was too shy of my body to flit naked

157

around the heath. With the time that had elapsed and the little that had changed, I was too embarrassed to call any of the friends who had reached out to me when I had returned to London in the first weeks of June. I took to phoning my mother more often, who accepted the sudden increase in calls with bewildered resentment. But no sooner did she open our conversations with the same gambit – So you remember me now, do you? – than I realised that unlocking my phone, scrolling through my contacts to the letter 'M', and punching the large green key of a circle with a picture of a phone in the middle was a catastrophic mistake of untold stupidity which could only serve to plunge me into regret: everything she said rang with disgusting amounts of logic and truth. Before calling my mother, I was an unhappy, failing adult. After calling my mother, I was an unhappy, failing child. You really over-complicate it for yourself, don't you? she sighed. You're wasting money living on a sofa and eating Pret a Manger when you could just commute from here. Come. Home.

It's a two-hour commute.

Sharp breath down the end of the line. It's an hour and a half, your father does it every weekday, only he does it north. Somehow it hasn't killed him. I don't see how it would kill you, it's the same amount of time you told me you spend walking to work.

I regretted telling her anything about my life, let alone the time it took me to walk to work. These walks were usually the time of day I called her, but now, it was a rainy weekend in mid-October. My flatmate was out to drinks with her friends. I had a lamp on and the sofa swaddled with sheets. The state of the pavements in

London is less of a disgrace than the National Rail service, I said sullenly. I don't want to spend four hours a day on cramped, dirty rush-hour trains that probably don't even run on schedule. I have other things to do.

You've told me you don't have any friends, my mother pointed out with alacrity. What else do you have to do? This was true, and it hurt. I want to be independent, I burst out. I want to have a life. I don't want to sit in my childhood bedroom and go to work like a zombie, and then do nothing.

Is that why you've been ignoring your father and me?

I kept quiet. I could hear her shrugging over the phone. I stayed with your grandparents until I was ready to get married, she said placidly. It didn't turn out so badly for me.

It was impossible to let her finish. I had heard this all before. I did not want to get married. I'm not getting married, I told her. I don't see how I could start an independent life for myself by getting married.

I don't see how you're able to save for a mortgage when you're sitting in cinemas every evening.

Don't be ridiculous, I snapped. My generation can't afford mortgages. Anyway, I have to go, I don't feel well.

She was quick with her concern; asked – What's wrong? I told her it was possible I was developing anxiety. She withdrew her concern: You don't have anxiety. I hung up the phone. I resolved, for the umpteenth time that week, not to call her again but it was too late. Not satisfied at the abruptness of the conversation's end, and now used to being in touch, she rang me. I ignored the call and opened a browser; I took my unhappiness into my own hands. Not my mother dispensing it, but the news instead, the Home Secretary standing at a lectern and declaring an Australian-style, points-based immigration system: *This daughter of immigrants needs no lectures from the north London, metropolitan, liberal elite.*

I heard the key turning in the door and knocked the switch on the lamp to its off position; hid beneath the sheets. But my phone still issued the Home Secretary's speech. My flatmate paused incrementally over the sofa on her way to her room to listen. From the corridor: – Wrong news flow. You're behind. Parliament's called back again and the Benn Act's been passed. Before she reached her room, I switched the lamp back on. What else have I missed?

Her voice advanced. The PM sent two letters to Europe today. She came into the room and sat down on the sofa with me. One was an unsigned request for a Brexit extension, and the other was a signed letter arguing against it. She passed her phone to me and let me read an article on the matter myself. I squinted at the brightness of her screen.

Oh, I said. That's a bit like what happened at work.

She gave me an odd look; asked how so. I reminded her of the article about landed climate change protesters and went on: the picture editor and art director had given the editor of the magazine two final proofs to pick. The first featured photos of one of the protests done by the organisers of the movement – red robes evangelising on the pavements and road that made up Westminster Bridge. The effect was striking. The organisers had painted their faces white, and even though it could not have been so, in the photos they looked utterly silent: palms extended, red fabric bleeding into red fabric, now swaying gently to lean upon each other, now raising flags above their ranks. It looked more like a fashion shoot than the actual fashion shoot, which had been sent out on the second version of the proof, shot in shades of greige. The landed protesters had refused to wear couture, deeming it at odds with their beliefs on the distribution of wealth. My flatmate snorted. Surely agreeing to be photographed for a society magazine was already at odds with a view to distributing wealth? I nodded. Quite. Anyway, they'd hired models instead, with skin airbrushed to the colour and texture of apricots. They wore denim and knitwear, were arranged into a human pyramid, looked off into the middle distance. The art director had put her face in her hands when the photoshoot came back. Oh, fucking Christ, she moaned. What the fuck? At which point the picture editor, clearly having anticipated such a result, unearthed the protest photos she had pulled and suggested sending two versions. When the art director kept her head in her hands, the picture editor had printed them out and shoved them between her elbows. Look, she said, we'll put our signature on the one with the protest photos and send it along with the photoshoot one, and see which one he signs off on.

And? my flatmate asked.

He sent both back, the one with the real photos untouched, the photoshoot one signed.

She looked at the article on her phone again. That's a bit ridiculous, don't you think? I didn't bother to ask which bit she meant and said nothing. I don't want to put you out, she said finally, but you're finishing your job at the end of this month anyway and you can't live on my sofa forever. I'm not exactly happy at the tension it's been creating over the past couple of weeks.

I nodded. She sighed again.

I'm sorry for being a bit uptight. But I need you to apologise for infringing my personal boundaries too, okay?

I apologised. She patted me on the knee. Don't worry about bills for this month. Just find somewhere for November onwards, okay?

It was a relief, almost. I let my head loll on the armrest and listened to her tell me about her night: how she'd arrived late because customers wouldn't leave the bookshop after its closing; how the guy she liked had bought her three pints of Guinness. At some point I fell asleep.

After my last day at work, I took my sheets off the sofa. There had been no fanfare at the office; I had barely needed to say goodbye. Leaving was complicated only by the detritus on my desk. I had accrued mugs, books, boxes of tea, spare shoes in my drawer, umbrellas, hairbands, hand creams, lip balms and various other beauty freebies that got delivered to the office for magazine staff. Also, energy bars, plasters, wooden chopsticks wrapped in thin, translucent paper, a coin purse with 80p in it, a few reusable plastic bags. It was like moving out of a house in miniature. Emptying my flatmate's living room of my things was less so.

In the end, I could not say goodbye to her. The election had been announced and she went straight from work to canvassing doorsteps. She left a note: *Good luck, please leave the fob and house keys on the dining room table*. I texted before I left to ask how it was going and what time she'd be back. Not till late, don't wait up, was the reply. Canvassing was hard. No one wanted you on their front door. No one wanted a reminder of the state of the nation anywhere near their house unless it was insubstantial, on a screen. Please could I be gone early tomorrow morning, as we'd agreed? She wanted to use her living room as a base for Labour members in her area to strategise. I wrote back, Of course, and began googling the election. I watched a clip from the previous day's PMQs and struggled to keep up. I read an op-ed in *The Times* on the leader of the opposition and the fractiousness of his party. I read the Prime Minister's Twitter feed. I felt shock at how laborious it was, to be fully up to date with the news. I was ostensibly unemployed, but an afternoon of research felt like its own full-time job.

How possible was it to stay wilfully attuned without living in permanent fear or guilt? The very phone one kept up to speed with existed only by the unheard suffering of others. I read an article which pointed out the fact that any egalitarianism of digital culture rested on the exploitation of Navajo women in early electronic manufacture. I drank a litre of water and read another article on the exploitation of Facebook moderators who watched thousands of hours of traumatising material to make sure others didn't. I turned my phone off and put it on the other side of the room. I went into my flatmate's room and watered her cacti; I thought of all the names for rose breeds I knew, *floribunda*, *grandiflora*, *rambling*, *centifolia*. I wondered if, to keep on good terms with her in case I ever needed something in the future, there was a hardy enough rose plant I could offer that would survive in the kitchen's window box. I turned my phone back on in the interest of googling – but the season was all wrong: even the gardening community on Twitter had the election on their mind. A kindly man from Northumberland finally told me the roses weren't likely to thrive in the cold. I tried to separate the disappointment I felt about this news from the impulse to hate him and logged off. I wanted to think it was exhausting, but on account of the abused workers I had just read about, couldn't. I called my mother instead. I'm coming back, I said.

PART THREE

'I, who am driven mad
By my ideas, who go nowhere'

III.N

London, framed by rising white columns. The last of October; the grey. The traffic on Millbank, and the Thames, seeping. It had turned autumn. Beyond the portico under which I stood, there was rain. I could envisage it further out beyond where I was, pouring plashless over Big Ben, over statues, over Westminster – slick and patterning the city's corsets, the pipe iron casings around clock and Parliament, holding them in and lacing them up. And here, from the steps of Tate Britain, from its square of pillars for anyone to observe: the 87 bus on its rounds. The rushing red body; the black leather whirling round the pavement. Some streaks of rain-dashed colour shone on the road below it: rainbows hovering on black tar, itself brushed and covered by the leaves which had departed their boughs – wizened past season, adding orange to the mix. Those bursts of colour in covert gleams, here and there between the city's uniformity, its colour of chalky stone, of colleges, of embassies; towards the Thames, the colour of glass, silver high-rises over silver water. I shook my umbrella out to it all, heaved my suit-case onto the museum's virgin floor. I made the first wet tracks. 10 a.m.: opening hour. A woman wearing a lanyard offered me a cloakroom. I could not say yes. I gripped the long metal hook trundling my case, but she, firm – You really can't take it in there.

I felt argumentative. Well, why not? Because it obstructed the floor space in the galleries for other visitors. I looked around: it was 10 a.m. on a Thursday, there were no other visitors. Yes, but there would be. Ah, I said, well, what if I left before it got crowded? It was like Wimbledon, but out of season and for petty admin. Her backhand was impeccable. If I did not leave my items in the cloakroom, I would have to leave. We smiled at each other. I submitted to her. I expected her eyes to follow me: heading left, past the paintings from the 1930s and towards the Clore Gallery, but beyond the matter of my luggage she did not care about me. I passed through unwatched.

The clatter-click of my shoes went acoustic on the Clore Gallery floor; started low, wood panelling emitting the odd squeak, then opened out, embraced the curved white ceiling and bounced off burgundy walls. I stood at the foot of its main corridor. The casings to each room had no doors, were twice the size and fit of regular doors, and devoid of any sense of entry or exit. The point was just to create a break in the walls, which themselves existed only for the paintings: to group them by subject and give them their place; to hold them aloft for each museum-goer's staring face. People began to drift through. I could spy on them at an angle through the gaps in the walls. They were pensioners and groups of schoolchildren in neon jackets. They were artists setting up easels in front of their chosen paintings.

I knew I did not have long before some man's maddening phone was pushed in front of every canvas I wanted to see. I took the first room on the left. The walls there were the shade of a pigeon's underbelly: three paintings affixed to each, and a fat little bench with short legs and a puff of quilted red leather split into six seats in the centre of everything. A greying man with a waxed hooded jacket listening to his wireless through earphones was already on it: the wireless was turned up to maximum sound. From the seat's left side you could hear, in digest, a Bronze Age monument discovered in the Forest of Dean; the Grenfell Tower Inquiry Phase 1 Report; a reminder of the upcoming general election; placations from Number 10 about the Brexit delay. I took the middle of the bench. The Tate was refuge, procrastination; I had however long the museum's Turner collection lasted me before I ran out of reasons to catch a train out of London. I closed my eyes. The backs of my lids lit up with little rainbow squares: they were like the pavement – the colours dived and fluttered. The little tin sound of public radio came through like an earworm. It was the chart-topping song I couldn't get away from. The country, going to shit: played over and over on everyone's electronic devices. I squeezed my eyes tighter.

When I opened them again, there was Devonshire in a heavy bronze frame, and two black-coated men in their twenties in front of it. I took them in. Cloth tote bags, woollen beanies, exposed ankles and old socks in their clean white shoes. One of them rolled a cigarette while the other proselytised.

Of course, that's the grand irony of referring to Turner as a British artist. He paused to allow his companion time to lick along the length of the cigarette's Rizla; the fag was sealed with a flourish, and then, when he was sure of his friend's undivided attention, the proselytising continued. All of this stuff is essentially Italianate. And his best work, as far as this museum is concerned, is in the other room: the studies of light in France and Belgium. Of the ports. Those paintings have a sense of *motion*. He grew animated. They are the product of advancing technologies – steam power; the increasing availability of travel. See the magnificence such availability brought.

To me it seemed his companion was bored because it sounded as though his friend was quoting from a catalogue – in any event, he shrugged. He had a German accent in contrast to his friend's RP, but like his companion, his clothes were pure London. I do not know, he said. These paintings will be on your country's banknotes soon, no? Clearly they still have some nationalist value. Then seeing the frown on his friend's face, added, Shall we see the ones you like again before I go and smoke this?

They went on strolling the perimeter of the room until they found the gap in the wall.

Unseeing their words took time. It was labour to regain the canvas, to extract the hipster-beanie-art-school-craft-beer pallor overlaid on the image. As an extra precaution, I took my phone out intending to listen to white noise through my earphones: instead I found an iCloud notification; two missed calls from my mother. I ignored the calls and swiped the notification instead. My phone's photo gallery appeared, rearranged with a line of white sans-serif text over it that read, *One year ago*. The room I'd rented in Bradmore Road with ten cardboard boxes and a suitcase yet unpacked; various close-ups of carpet stains, cracks in the walls and the scuffs on the wooden armrests of an easy chair to be noted in inventory. To which my phone: *Would you like to share this memory?* Over a year ago, flattened out into pixels on my screen and being callously replayed. I remembered the unpacking, the wasps on the windows. How late last year's summer had stayed. I had reached the point where my days at Bradmore began to lay themselves under new ones; had acquired the perfectly poignant distance of 365 days. I was not ready to feel it, it was too painful. I stuffed my phone back in my pocket.

Devonshire on a wall. If I had closed my eyes again, I would have been able to place myself in it, but to do so would mean not looking at the painting again. I looked. For the first ten minutes all I could think of was cigarette smoke: Turner's clouds travelling to the left of the canvas in rising spirals. At the bottom of the painting was a brook, and two figures in it. There was another at its edge. I did not want the implication of another person's thought. I ignored them. I wanted something else – to see the painting as it truly was; to have a landscape in my mind's eye, alone.

First the brook: it had no breadth; it ran umber in foreshortened depth. The bed of water bled into the bank and out of it. Two tree trunks slashed into the foreground's left; on the right, a set of shrubs laced the beginnings of a forest. Then, between the curtain of rising bough-bends, the foliage thickening upwards, another body of water in the background, centre-left, streaming out towards more green. There was a viaduct loping from one wall of trees to the next, and at its end, a stucco house with yellow walls and peeling white stains, with frail, blown-out draperies: a lemon-sherbet treat of a thing in its wrinkling paper bag. Half hidden beyond it, encased in English countryside, I could see a glimpse of abstract buildings; a town. But this did not stir in me the same feeling that the landscape did. I was done with towns, with cities. Further back, before the sky broke the land, after yet more green stippled into the distance before it – I did not know why I thought it was, only that it must be – the Channel. Only after having looked at the land did the clouds become something else: idyllic, hung in blemishless English sky.

I looked for long enough to understand the initial impulse to climb inside. There was a clearing in the forest, carved and deepening beyond the suggestion of paint; there was shading down the inside of the viaduct's furthermost parapet, it hinted at pavement that could be walked on. There was a set of boulders by the brook's edge on which to sit – numerous places within the painting to reside. I felt, unexpectedly and in my chest, a kind of swelling, a sense of pleasure, or fantasy enjoyment. For a moment, in my head, it was summer, and I could have been on some green with a picnic basket for luggage and the sound of wrens over babbling water. I could have been biting into a Braeburn or reclining in a gentle breeze. Then a woman walked in front of my frame. I scowled, but she wasn't facing me; she was leaning back to get my landscape into her phone. When she had finished, she leaned over the museum label to the left of the frame. I could have killed her.

I did not. At some point, the man with the wireless radio had left. There was a whole new turnover of people in the room. I checked my phone. I had been there for half an hour, it seemed reasonable to look at something else. A palate cleanser. On my phone's screen, Twitter had sent me an 'in case you missed it' notification: I opened it. There was my corner of the internet, ironic, cackling with glee, *Happy Brexit Day*. I allowed myself a moment of smugness, too, at the failure of the venture. Further down, there was more on the implications of a second referendum; which party was for a people's vote and which one against, which party opposed the prospect of no-deal, but the joy I had felt began to leak out of me. I tried to regain it in front of another canvas and realised with horror that what I had felt earlier was patriotism. I could more clearly identify it now: the canvas was all ochre and verdant lea with rushed scruffs of paint for trees – there was no sun, but there was a lightening in the blue sky, a patch of yellowish white, orb-shaped. Somewhere in the centre of that was a turreted grey mass, the suggestion of a crumbling manor. The whole thing was abstract enough in style to take on whatever you gave it; and so, though it was unmistakably English, it could have been Yorkshire, it could have been Sussex, it could have been the view of the fields off the M25 around Hertfordshire. Whatever bit of English countryside you could connect it to in your head took hold, and because the painting was a beautiful thing, with its warm tint, its heavy golden frame and its place in the airy, magnificent gallery, the country became beautiful, too.

After this realisation, I could not enjoy the pleasure I felt looking at a room full of Turners. But nor could I quash it. When I looked at the tangled fields, a chorus of associations independent of my own wishes struck up in my head: Heathcliff, looking out across the moor for his love; Lizzie Bennet against the backdrop of Netherfield, in stubborn refusal of hers. All of it was compounded by the lushness of period dramas the original materials had sprung. The BBC had a lot to answer for. I was newly uncomfortable in the gallery, but I did not want to leave. For the first time since I had had my own room in Oxford, walking through the gallery conferred a mode of solitude in which I could figure out what I thought, what that made me, and how I had arrived at the things I did. Because the room I was in did not belong to me, I could not do this infinitely. But for the moment I was in it at least, I had the dignity and freedom of a sense of self which belonged entirely to me. I wanted to keep it. I reflected. I could not be like Ghislane, who did not care about the permanence or strength or stability of such things; who had no bodily self and was happy to transmit herself through photos, or a song, or on a page. I could not be like the intern, who compromised to a fault; managed on only espressos for lunch and the hope they would sell a coat to make up for poor wages – all that to cling to a place to which they only tenuously belonged. Where I was going, I would still have to share the bathroom; be conscious of the length of my showers; suffer interruptions of thought if I had to make breakfast in the kitchen, or explain where I had been after leaving the house. Despite my discomfort, I wanted to stay in the Clore Gallery a moment longer.

To resolve this, I thought it best to try to notice what was false in each painting, and by extension, in my own feelings. I began to feel restless; forced myself to move to the next one. This time, I did not marvel at the suggestion of vetiver on the banks of a stream, the willows bending over it and the clear azure sweep near the top of the frame. I looked up.

The Clore Gallery lit its rooms with strips of rectangular light lined flat into the ceiling, and though this would have been ugly under any circumstance, after the general majesty of what was below, it seemed an affront. Now that the light was ugly, I followed it down. The piece I was stood in front of had a heavy, ornate frame with the painting's catalogue number, title and year carved into it. Parts of it shone more brightly than others: certain groves were deliberately blackened to give an even greater impression of depth.

A woman in a face mask came next to me. I switched my attention to her: she too was a part of the painting now; made up the experience of looking at it. She ignored me; looked briefly at the label, took a picture; then, clearly uncomfortable with being looked at, left. I went back to my original view. I could see the weft of the fabric. It bobbled the pastoral landscape; divided it up into little patches and squares. There was a rip in the canvas that bulged beyond the paint.

It was impossible to look at anything like this for long. It required constant vigilance. With its joylessness, its state of compulsory paranoia, I became less of a person. And then there was the fact of my attention: overripe with two hours spent in the gallery and in need of rest. I might have taken myself to lunch, except I could not justify spending what it would cost to sit in one of the museum's restaurants or cafes. There were more missed calls from my mother on my phone. And at some point or another, I would have to collect my suitcase from the cloakroom. I resigned myself to leaving.

Squeezing my case between the aisle and seats on the 9 and 87 bus had been awkward enough in the morning, on the way in. I did not want to do it again. I also did not want to lug the thing to Pimlico; to hoist it gracelessly down the Underground, past the barriers, the escalators; to grip it constantly, and keep it from sliding around the Tube. Despite my reservations about lunch, or perhaps because of them, and my increasingly insistent hunger, I wanted comfort. I got an Uber.

The car that arrived was clean enough to eradicate any suggestion of a personality. Before I got in it I could hear the driver's playlist coming through over the speakers and towards the back seat, but once he had put my suitcase in the boot and we were settled in, he turned it off and lowered the volume on the navigation app displayed on his phone, too. The silence was stultifying. I did not want to force inane conversation, and yet I felt it reflected badly to seem indifferent towards the person who was performing a service for me. The car was a small one. The proximity of space, coupled with the aspect of antisocialness my sitting in the back had induced, was made all the more terrible by lack of sound. I asked how his day was.

Not bad, he said. The silence went on, difficult, as it had been before. I didn't want to, but I tried again. Busy day?

Not really, he said. It had been a slow, boring morning, though he had been intrigued by the idea of a pickup from the Tate. Was I an artist? I told him no. Oh, that's a shame, he said. He was keen to talk artists as of late. His girlfriend was one: they had been having an ongoing disagreement over something she had read. The very gallery I had been in was advertising a job in one of their coffee shops for 5K more than its curators made. I leaned forward. Where had she found that?

Twitter, he said. He might have been able to discuss this with his girlfriend's friends, but apart from one day off yesterday, work had kept him away. He would not be able to do so for a few more days. I nodded; plugged his keywords into my phone. On Twitter, a well-known progressive artist had retweeted a photo of a column from *The Times*, which read, *The daily grind is better rewarded at the Tate galleries if you're in hospitality rather than something as trivial as art. The Tate is seeking a 'head of coffee', for which it is offering a salary of £39,500. That is £5,000 more than it pays its current exhibition curators. The advert says it is seeking someone with 'extensive experience of cupping'. Presumably they don't require customers to cough while they do it.* Above it, the artist himself had written, *I give up, they've won.* I read this all to the driver while he turned off the Victoria Embankment and towards the Strand. We hit traffic near Kingsway.

No, I don't know who that is, he said once I had given him the artist's name. But the conversation he'd been having with his girlfriend was about perceived value in the traditional sense. I asked him what he meant. His girlfriend had not liked the disparity in salary between restaurant staff, whom she saw as unskilled workers, and curators, who, by her implication, were skilled. *The*

Times column I had just read had done the same thing by implying the coffee job was 'trivial', or, at least, more trivial than working in the arts. This, he disagreed with. Despite the silliness of the ad, the strange HR-ification of the job title designed to make essentially boring work sound fun, what was being advertised was a high-pressure, front-of-house managerial job, which required time-management skills, efficiency, a way with people, and a detailed knowledge of a particular beverage industry. He had told his girlfriend there was more pride and practical use to be found in a job like this than in any of the posturing and simpering and affectation he saw in the art world.

He shrugged. Understandably, she had taken offence. But he stood by it. The whole argument was stupidly middle class in tone. Yet, in his ends, people who did service work were often underpaid and badly treated. He would take his stance on the difference in pay between gallery and food service staff to his grave. On the other hand, he regretted the irony of the fact that the gig work he was doing now meant he could not resolve the rift this stance had created in his relationship. Having heard one thing, his girlfriend was now finding it difficult to believe that he had not been belittling *her* job. He had just been standing up for ones like his.

I nodded. That was understandable. Where were his ends? Where was he from?

Notting Dale. His eyes flicked up to the rear-view mirror, searching for any sign of recognition and then back to the road. I shook my head. He went on: close by the Grenfell Tower. And catching my eyes again, added that he was not there any more.

By now we were at Holborn. My stomach dropped, churned. Had he read the inquiry report? He had. Had I? I had not.

It had taken him all day yesterday. He'd felt duty-bound to do it. The report was more than eight hundred pages long, and truthfully, a lot of it blurred in his mind. He'd skipped around a bit. Some parts were very technical, showed spandrel locations and sloping angles; noted the burning rate of combustible synthetics found in the cladding. There were graphs and photos of the estate from the year it had been built: construction frames climbing half-assembled rooms and window frames with computer-generated arrows drawn on them. It was beyond his reach to picture what was once some-one's home as foam insulation and beams, or as 'fig.1', with JPEG arrows overlaid. But the report also contained photos from inside the tower after the fire. At this point, he had stopped for a moment and wept. There had been a diagram of the kitchen where it had started, and over the impersonal, bureaucratic floor plan, its occupant had made some additions in blocky, elegant biro: labelled the number of cupboards, the location of the smoke alarm; the extent of the smoke when he had first seen it, light and white in colour.

When the Uber driver had resumed reading, a lot of the survivor testimony had induced second-hand fear in him – descriptions of occupants fighting for breath; running back for their family; telling the operators on 999 they were scared. But other parts of the report, for reasons he could not unpick, had felt devastating. One survivor had described the heat in her living room as similar to the heat you feel when you take a cake out of the oven. In the testimony of firefighters and 999 calls going through the control room, there were repeated variations on the advice given to occupants that they wet blankets, bedding and towels as defence strategy against the smoke: the image of all the repurposed, sodden cloth had set him off crying again. There was the fact that the witness testimony included repeated descriptions of the ventilation fans throughout the building humming in response to the fire; quiet, haunting groaning. The report described the failure of various domestic structures within each home in the building. The intensity of the heat from the fire was such that the windows failed, allowing the flames to penetrate the flats. The extractor fan units in the kitchens had nearly all deformed and dislodged, providing the flames another point of entry. The fire doors did not hold back smoke, or lacked effective self-closing devices.

He turned into the taxi ramp at Euston. I made no move to get out. Finally, he exhaled. More than anything, he had cried at the number of preventable deaths caused by the instruction given on the night, that residents would be safest if they stayed put inside their homes. Some people did not understand that in this country, you had to be a particular type of person to always be safe at home. At the end of the report, when it was done, he had gone out; driven up and down the A40 near the tower block multiple times. Two years on. He was tired. He had seen Grenfell, now covered with some kind of grey sheet; a banner on top: *Forever in Our Hearts*. He wished whoever it was who'd put it there – the estate, the borough council, the government – had had the courage to leave the building exposed: incised into people's eyes and buckling the expression on their faces, where it could not be ignored. What good was it to store something like that away in a place as private and messy and ineffectual as the heart? The human cost, the class snobbery, the neglect of the thing. The grey sheet showed that the most important thing to the inhabitants of this city was its veneer: that things should look okay, even if they weren't. He wanted that tower to mean something else. He wanted that burnt-out, blackened husk to disturb the genteel, white buildings in Kensington and Whitehall. It did not. It stood tastefully covered up.

The cabs behind us began to sound their horns. The Uber driver swung himself out of the car and retrieved my suitcase from the boot. When I followed, he was taller than I expected, in turned-up jeans and a black fleece; with a swollen face and bags under his eyes. He looked apologetic – perhaps the conversation had been a bit much for two strangers on a short drive. On my part, the impulse to be polite crashed into the admiration and honesty I wanted to show him. We shook hands. While he held mine, he made a joke about giving me a five-star rating via the app on account of our therapy session.

Euston, not as large as it should have been. Euston, squat and hulking. There was the square outside the station: it had statues and pigeons looking for their lunch. It was all shades of grey and the curling fug of cigarette smoke, the strawberry-scented issue from vapes. People kept appearing suddenly and slowing my progress, tangling their suitcase with my suitcase, or else stopping entirely to stand in one place. I wanted to say, am I invisible to you? To the lady who had stepped directly in front of me to take a phone call. Out of all proportion, I wanted to tear off her face. In my stomach, there was the familiar, anxious poison of fear and bitterness.

Inside the station, I took a left. The automated machines. £13.25 for a yellow-and-orange ticket with font on it that belonged to an eighties computer game. After I'd shoved it into the back of my phone case, my neck craned up at the screen showing train times. Delayed. Well, of course. I had a book with me, but it was thin and I was already more than halfway through it: I had wanted to pass the time on the train by reading. With nothing else to do, I sat on my case. Out of unthinking habit, I checked my emails. The previous day, the managing editor had sent me a list of questions asking where on the shared hard drive fact checks and versions of proofs were, and I'd replied courteously, elated despite myself that I might still be needed, and things might fail without me. She had not emailed back. Not even in thanks. Leaving work was like being broken up with within a semi-abusive relationship. Today my inbox was empty. I sat on my case and pulled down refresh until I lost count.

When the platform number was announced for the train, the main body of the station and the ramps towards the platform began haemorrhaging. Things fell apart. It was mid-afternoon, and the station was crowded, but not particularly full. Yet travelling salesmen in leather shoes flew past voluptuously grouped families, past teenage girls with Primark shopping bags; jammed their tickets into the barrier gate; stabbed the open/close button on carriage doors like animals in pain. I noted all this with distaste. Then I noted my distaste. This was my main fear in leaving London. That a parochial habit of watching what other people did and a running commentary on their failings would lodge itself in my brain. That such commentary would become my main form of anecdote. I wanted, always, to maintain the metropolitan affect of never being fazed. I walked at normal pace to the very front of the train, and got into passenger car 'A'. Two other commuters followed. And once we had settled into the carriage space, chosen discrete corners in which to pass the journey, I took my coat off. I hoisted my luggage into the overhead compartment and saw a girl curled into a window seat with her shoes off and her feet on the furred green seats. She was propping her phone up against the bulk of a WH Smith bag on the grim plastic table in front of her, watching Netflix as though she were in bed with her earphones in. I saw another, slightly older woman near the end of the carriage, unwrapping an M&S sandwich and leaving it on the little table that folded down from the seat in front of her. She set aside her flapjack, bottle of water, put on her reading glasses, and began to look over a bundle of printed documents. She bit into the sandwich and started up her laptop on the seat next to her.

I dropped back into my chair. I wished I'd thought to buy a newspaper, or food; that I possessed whatever ability it was which made these women so able to create little nests of space wherever they were. The carriage shuddered, the conductor came on overhead. We began to move. London's outer boroughs, its rows of suburban housing, washed themselves in faded brown and grey over each window; peeled successively away in diminishing forms. I had my book. I tried to read but the words slid along the page, making no impression on my mind. I hadn't had lunch, and I was hungry. Each past sentence I read evaporated in my memory as soon as the next one took hold. The futility of the task was oppressive enough that when a call came from my mother, I took it, and prayed that at some point, the train would drive into a tunnel so that the signal would break the conversation off at a natural, early end. It turned out there was not much to do but listen. A new couple had moved in next door, and they were fuming on account of the Brexit delay, it was inadvisable to stop for a chat if I saw them on my way in. She herself had endured a very long, arduous conversation about the general election with them, and they'd assumed she voted their way. Then, my father had turned up, and by the sounds of his accent, it was very clear that she didn't. There was a palaver about apologising for the rude things they'd said about Remoaners: of course, by the looks of my father, in his suit, with his iPhone 10 and regional-accent-inflected English, there could be no question he paid his tax; worked as a valued member of the UK economy. My mother cackled down the phone. The English were too polite for convictions. By the way, there was a new housing development being built on the fields across the road, and so I might like to wear sensible shoes when I arrived, things were a bit muddy.

I said it was too late, I was already on the train and all I had were heels and fashionable trainers because I had just spent the last four months working at a society magazine in London. Outside, the scenery came to a stop; became Wembley, dispensing passengers and long whistle blows. Don't you raise your voice at me for it, my mother said, there was enough noise going on her end already. But I was having waking nightmares about being assaulted with mud, the sound of drills, of construction work, again. I thought the whole point of the countryside was that nothing ever happened in it, I said.

Yes, very droll, she said. There was a lot of construction happening all over, actually. People being priced out of London were moving into the villages and towns. There wasn't enough housing to keep up with the demand. The newer houses were expensive; full of modern technology built into the walls, but equally, there weren't enough amenities to keep up with the influx of population. The roads leading to the high street were consistently jammed. The schools were struggling to keep the number of pupils in classrooms down. Yesterday, she had waited half an hour at the checkouts in Morrisons, when a few years ago, she had only used to wait five minutes. I felt my eyes roll into the back of my head. Wembley unclenched from the window. Look, I feel awkward being the only passenger talking on the train, I said. I'll see you when I'm there. She called me poppet and said she was getting things ready for me before she hung up the phone. I pictured my mother dusting the mantelpiece with its framed family photos; going over the rugs with a vacuum and plumping the cushions so that they stood up against each other on the sofa, like little tents. I could hear her complaining to no one in particular that the dust from the construction was dirtying the windows, and felt tenderly towards her. I sent a warmer, love-laden text. I was not without shame.

The ticket inspector came into the train car with his ticket machine: the woman eating a meal deal from M&S showed him hers first. She had to pile her papers under her chin and shift her laptop, now balanced on her knees, awkwardly about to look for it. When at last she had pulled it out, the inspector nodded briefly, said, That's great, thanks, and continued on. It took enough time for the train to move in and out of Watford.

The girl at the window seat watching Netflix sat straight up, as though she'd been caught cheating on a test; swung her feet immediately off the seats and took her earphones out. She, too, showed him her ticket, and he gave a nod as he passed. Now, it was me. I had no bearings to collect. I flashed him the back of my phone. It took ten seconds: he peered at the card wedged between the device and the protective cover; he said, Nice one, as though my ticket had somehow been better than all the rest. He disappeared into the driver's compartment of the train. I went back to my book. I turned pages without reading. I looked out of the window again. We had travelled far enough out of London for the view to turn into pasture. England, the fat impasto of the land painted on faintly clouded Plexiglas, hung through a dirty rust-covered frame. I took it in. It had its own, terrible majesty. Dashed landscape rippling past me, shaken out like sheets over a bed, and the sky like a blade. The sight of it went through me. I could have been looking at my old nursery, or the first cot I ever lay in. Despite my efforts to feel the contrary, there was some sentiment attached. Tomorrow, in my mother's wellingtons, I would take a walk up hills and fields. Shortly after my leaving home, my parents had moved to a small market town. This was where I would be. I would be stomping over to where an iron sign announced its borders, black and official and brilliant and hard. I had a fascination with road and street signs like these, which looked like they had been made mid-century and then left out for the successive generations they guided. In the town where my parents lived, there was an absence of blue plaques, and an abundance of little black-and-white street signs. They pointed to the markets, the schools, the railway lines. I tried to imagine who I would be, as a result of this town. In however long it would take to find another job, I wanted to think I would turn fresh-faced after all the walks and good, sharp air. I would have time to cultivate habits impossible to sustain in London – I would cook whole, robust meals and read voraciously. I would make myself better. I began to daydream.

The doors in an imaginary house swung open. There was a kitchen, ranks of dried herbs, spices, legumes. Worktops, washing machine, boiler. I saw violets resting in a jug in the sink and hand soap in its dispenser. There was a living room, too, with ivy-coloured walls. Two sofas in the centre, facing each other, and a coffee table in between, piled with clutter: newspapers and stray pens. One bedroom, more or less filled with a double bed; a nondescript bathroom, remarkable only in that it was clean. I did not know who I shared the house with, but there were two toothbrushes under the mirror, on the sink; two sponges resting on the bath.

The reality was that it was drizzling and the train pulled up to its next stop. I'd closed my eyes – I knew this only because I had to open them. The girl with her feet on the seats watching Netflix was stuffing her shoes on. She wrapped her scarf around her and stepped onto the platform outside. By the way she kept her film streaming on the phone in her hand and her head bent towards it, it was clear: she knew where she was. The WH Smith bag dangled tidily off the crook of her wrist and knocked about her thigh. I craned my neck out for her. She was gone before the train left.

What had a rented room in Oxford and a sofa in London made me? Where had there been to make me? For all my plans, it seemed impossible I could achieve anything. There had been no place I could have dragged a sofa into, painted the walls whatever colour I wanted, stayed in long enough to find inviting colleagues over for dinner and drinks a worthwhile task. I had not found a job with which I could afford to put my life in one place, then nurture my relationship with family and friends. Yet somehow, I had spent the year keeping my possessions, temporarily, in what were ostensibly the highest echelons the country had to offer. I had even felt a sense of ownership over each building, granted by the access various keys, fobs and magnetised cards I had carried for them. There was humiliation attached to the feeling that these buildings were no longer mine. Had probably never been mine. I pictured my parents' house: the architectural and interior design opposite of everything I would have chosen for myself. It would not be mine, either. I thought of the last time I had been to stay. It was a house with thin walls. During the night, I had heard my parents turning in their bed; my father's whistling snore and my mother's gentle breathing. In the morning I had woken them up by closing the front door too loudly when I went out for a run at six. I had irritated them by buying impossible quantities of bread which were invariably left in the cupboards to mould past the time I left. Now, I did not even have a set of house keys.

Don't worry, my mother said when I texted her, you can use the spare set here. What had happened to mine? Well, mine *were* the spare set. I had scarcely been home. She had seen no reason not to lend them to guests, or the neighbours when she and my father went on holiday and the plants needed watering. It was true, but it did not stop me from feeling offended. I sent the thumbs up emoji. I wanted to put my phone away but my mother did not know that the thumbs up emoji constituted the end of a conversation in text. She had questions. Would I be looking for another job? If I found one, would I be moving back to London? I was welcome to stay however long I wanted, but if it was temporary, how long did I think I would be? The guilt mechanism permanently embedded in my head thrust the conversation I'd had with the Uber driver to the forefront of my head and how not twenty minutes ago I had been ashamed of the way I treated her – but I was bad-tempered and hungry, and most of all, I was tired. I switched my phone off.

Other than the view from the window, all there was to look at was the train carriage. There were two of us left in it. The woman with the laptop and printed papers had finished her M&S sandwich and flapjack dessert – at some point, she had got up and squashed them into a small metal bin built into one of the seats. The bin itself either had not been emptied regularly enough or was too small for the litter generated by the number of seats the carriage contained. The triangular cardboard smeared with lettuce leaves and mayonnaise poked out of it; there was a lid attached to the bin on a stiff hinge, it disfigured the rubbish it clamped down on and made the whole effect worse.

The more I looked, the more disgusting the carriage grew. There was a faint layer of brown on each of the brightly patterned seats, stretching upwards and becoming more concentrated at the headrests. I drew my head instinctively away from mine. It was impossible not to picture how many years and numbers of passengers sitting down would have to pass, and how long the seats would have to go without being cleaned, to build up that noticeable layer of brown. How could anyone sit comfortably once they had seen this? And how, without standing, could I rearrange myself so that I came into as little contact with that layer of brown as possible? I took my coat off the seat next to me and put it back on as a protective layer. As much as I could, I raised my back and my thighs off the chair so that the only part of me still on it was my behind, but this soon turned into a hellish form of public transport yoga. My limbs went heavy. I fell back into the seat.

It was impossible to slow the turn of my mind. The countryside cast itself past me, never the same from one second to the next. I tried looking out of the other windows in the passenger car so that it whipped by twice, in different perspectives. I tried to focus on my book, looked at the page – *but after reading a chapter or two a shadow seemed to lie across the page. It was a straight dark bar, a shadow shaped something like the letter 'I'.*

The train began to slow at another stop where the tracks had not been built far enough from the trees. A succession of branches slid up against the window until we came to rest, and then the wind drew them backwards and forwards: each bough, tapping against the carriage like a heartbeat. The other woman, my last companion in the passenger car, gathered her coat and bag; stood up; exited the train.

All year there had been a sound rising in me, I had never said it right. I stood up and over the stained seats, the smeared windows, into the carriage, screamed – *I*

The train moved off again. I jolted with it. The sound I had made broke round the empty space without use; waited, for the next stop to be home.

Author's Note

Three Rooms is a novel about the danger of withholding capital, principally domestic and financial. Through the unconditional faith and care of a large cohort of people, I have been the beneficiary of both while writing this book, and of much love.

To my parents, who did not bat an eye when I left my job and holed up in their house to write a book that might have amounted to nothing at all – I love you. Dziękuje też mojej babci. Część tej książki została napisana u Ciebie, na wsi. Czuję w niej Twoją miłość.

Thom Insley, Sophie Haydock, Charlie Selvaggi-Castelletti, Benjamin Wood, Nicole Seredenko, Alice Bonomini Borges: whether in part, or in full, you read it first, and kept me going. I owe you drinks. Serena Buccoliero, Rosy Cooley, Sveva Scenarelli: before, during and after my writing this book, you've always made sure I had a home with you. I will always do the same in turn.

To Dredheza Maloku, Ana Fletcher, Naomi Gibbs and Harriet Moore…you've changed my life completely. My first room of my own, the ability to do what I love, is down to your kindness and commitment. For that, and to everyone at Jonathan Cape, Houghton Mifflin Harcourt and David Higham, I am immeasurably and eternally yours.

Finally, quotations can be found throughout from Walter Pater's *The Renaissance*, Rosemary Tonks's 'The Sofas, Fogs, and Cinemas' and Virginia Woolf's *A Room of One's Own*. I am also incredibly grateful to Hannah Sullivan, whose *Three Poems* and 'Tenants' instructed my work, and whose emails have shown invaluable patience and support. Further acknowledgements go to the *LRB* classifieds, articles from *The Times*, *Tatler* and the *Guardian*, Sting and the Police, the inventiveness of protesters holding signs at the anti-Brexit march of 2019, members of the Memory Lane Facebook page, and the testimony which makes up the Grenfell Fire Inquiry Phase 1 Report. Transcriptions, personally made, from the 2019 Conservative Party leadership election have also been used.

penguin.co.uk/vintage